'Are you there, Katie?'

'I'm here, Peter,' she said, licking her lips to ease the dryness. 'I'll be here all night.'

And as she made the pledge she knew that, if he had heard it, he would see it as a sign of her devotion to duty—this all-night stint at the radio when a second cyclone was approaching Rainbow Bay.

But he didn't know about the other cyclone, she reminded herself. And he certainly didn't—and wouldn't—know that her 'devotion' might be to him, not duty!

That was something he would never know!

Having pursued many careers—from school-teaching to pig farming—with varying degrees of success and plenty of enjoyment, **Meredith Webber** seized on the arrival of a computer in her house as an excuse to turn to what had always been a secret urge—writing. As she had more doctors and nurses in the family than any other professional people, the medical romance seemed the way to go! Meredith lives on the Gold Coast of Queensland, with her husband and teenage son.

Recent titles by the same author:

WINGS OF PASSION
WINGS OF DUTY
COURTING DR GROVES
PRACTICE IN THE CLOUDS
FLIGHT INTO LOVE

WINGS OF
CARE

BY
MEREDITH WEBBER

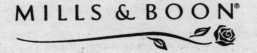

*All the characters in this book have no existence outside the imagina-
tion of the author, and have no relation whatsoever to anyone bearing
the same name or names. They are not even distantly inspired by any
individual known or unknown to the author, and all the incidents are
pure invention.*

*First published in Great Britain 1997
Harlequin Mills & Boon Limited,
Eton House, 18-24 Paradise Road, Richmond, Surrey TW9 1SR*

© Meredith Webber 1997

ISBN 0 263 80079 2

*Set in Times 10 on 11 pt. by
Rowland Phototypesetting Limited
Bury St Edmunds, Suffolk*

03-9704-53881-D

*Printed and bound in Great Britain
by Mackays of Chatham PLC, Chatham*

CHAPTER ONE

'*KATIE WATSON, Chief Radio Operator, Royal Flying Doctor Base, Rainbow Bay.*'

Katie smiled at the small, gold-lettered name-plate Peter Flint had presented to her when the office renovations had improved her desk space. She twirled the dials on the radio absent-mindedly, thinking of Peter and of silly adolescent dreams that wouldn't go away although she was now 'grown up'. . .

The strident blare of the Klaxon startled her back into attentive awareness. It was part of her job to know what was happening with the weather in their area.

'This cyclone warning is for Rainbow Bay and surrounding coastal districts,' she called to Jack Gregory, who was swearing under his breath at a computer on the table behind her. 'I've been listening for the one called Willie over in the gulf, but this is a new warning.'

'Willie's a stupid name for a cyclone,' Jack grumbled, transferring his disgust with the computer to the anonymous cyclone-namers at the weather bureau.

The warning noise ceased, and they both leaned forward a little to listen to the report that would follow.

'Category Two. . . Moving south-south-west at fifteen kilometres an hour. . . Wind gusts of up to 170 kilometres an hour. . . On present course could cross the coast near Rainbow Bay at midnight.'

'It'll veer away,' Katie said confidently, switching off the usual advice about torches and supplies of fresh water that would follow the prediction. She looked out

5

of the western window, where blue skies made mockery of the warning.

'Let's hope it will veer away,' Jack amended. 'The bureau's had an eye on a tropical low out in the Coral Sea for a few days now. It must have deepened to cyclone strength and picked up speed. The wind's pretty strong out there already and you can see a thick bank of cloud approaching from the east. Have you heard from Eddie or Peter? Are they on their way home?'

Katie smiled at the concern in Jack's voice. The Rainbow Bay base of the Royal Flying Doctor Service was his life and, as the senior medical officer, he clucked over the staff like a mother hen over her chickens.

'Peter radioed in earlier to say the Coorawalla phones were out, which is why I'm hovering by the radio instead of doing some of Leonie's filing. Eddie will call when they're in the air and he knows their ETA.'

'Coorawalla has radio phones, doesn't it?' Jack asked, and Katie's smile broadened. No one could deny that Jack was a wonderful doctor but even simple mechanical things, like radios and cellular phones, were a source of confusion to him, while the office computers were viewed as arch-enemies!

'And don't smile,' he said reprovingly. 'All I want to know is why our radio can remain in contact with them if their radio phone is out.'

'Their radio phone needs a high mast,' Katie explained, her lips still twitching. 'And with the wind gusts they've been experiencing, and the heavy rain, their tower must have been damaged. The HF radio they've kept at the hospital for back-up can be maintained with a bit of wire about forty metres long, strung out along the ground if necessary.'

'So they *are* having a bit of weather?'

Katie nodded. 'There's been a cyclone watch on Willie up there for three days. He's approaching from the north-west, and so far all he's done is whip up monstrous seas along the northern coastline and taunt the small communities in the gulf by changing direction every six hours.'

'And now?' Jack asked.

'I'll ring the bureau and check. Last time I heard he had turned south and was heading for Coorawalla, but it could be another false alarm.'

'Eddie will be getting the latest reports on Willie from Darwin, but will he know about the alert back here?' Jack asked, worrying at the question like a dog at his bone. 'If this new cyclone keeps heading towards the Bay he might fly out of Coorawalla and into worse weather on this side of the cape.'

He crossed to the large wall map that showed the area covered by their base and frowned as he traced his finger from the tiny island of Coorawalla across the land mass of the cape to the red star which denoted Rainbow Bay.

'Eddie will know what's going on, Jack,' Katie reminded him. 'It's the wet season, remember. Double cyclone alerts aren't uncommon at this time of the year. I wonder what they'll call the one heading our way?'

Would he guess that she was trying to divert his attention so that he wouldn't continue to brood on the safety of the employees at Coorawalla?

'Not Katie!' he said, turning from the map and smiling. 'You're the quiet, soothing type—not cyclonic at all.'

'Dead boring, you mean!' She flicked back her long straight hair and looked him straight in the eye.

Jack frowned as if the words she'd used to describe herself had startled him.

'No way!' he protested. 'Quiet and self-effacing, maybe, but very efficient. You must realise you're the rock we depend on when all hell breaks loose around this place.'

'Leonie Cooper is the rock you depend on,' Katie pointed out. 'She's the one who keeps the base running smoothly.'

They were still discussing the base manager when the radio called up their signal.

'It's Peter, Katie,' the disembodied voice announced. 'Eddie and Susan are on their way home. They've got Janet Nupoota with them. She's experiencing severe headaches, stomach pains—but no vomiting—and general debility. Tell Jack I'm stumped. I'm sending her back to the Bay so they can do more exhaustive tests in hospital.'

Jack rolled his chair across to the radio desk, signalling to Katie that he would reply. She pushed her chair clear of the radio and logged the conversation, noting down the time and leaving a space for the ETA which Eddie would soon provide.

Eddie and Susan, and soon Nick and Allysha! There would be two married couples at the Base. Was having a husband-and-wife team on the same flight a good idea? she wondered idly. Susan, a flight sister, had met Eddie Stone, their chief pilot, when she began working with the Service many years ago. Now that their twins were teenagers, and could be left overnight, they enjoyed working together once again. But if they were held up somewhere—

She forgot these minor concerns as she heard Jack ask Peter, 'How come the plane's on its way home and you're still there?'

Across five hundred kilometres of land and sea Katie imagined that she could feel Peter's reaction. He wouldn't have stayed at Coorawalla on a whim, particularly with a cyclone on the way!

'As you know, Janet's the only trained medical person on the island, apart from an aide, and as I've sent her across to the mainland I felt obligated to stay,' he explained. 'If Cyclone Willie does hit the community, there could be injuries that need immediate attention. Even with the best will in the world, disaster response teams won't be able to fly in until the winds abate and the airstrip is cleared.'

Katie watched Jack shift uncomfortably in his chair. He would have made the same choice, she knew, but that wouldn't diminish his concern for Peter's safety.

'Coorawalla Hospital is new enough to have been built to cyclone standards, isn't it?' he asked.

'You know it is, Jack!' Peter said, and chuckled as if he understood exactly how his boss was feeling. 'As soon as I'm off the phone I'm going to shift the three patients, all the necessary cyclone safety gear and the radio into the central core and stay there, so don't worry about me. If you want a problem,' he added, 'give some thought to Janet's symptoms. I'm sending her for tests, but the other reason I'm staying is that I've two kids in the hospital with similar symptoms.'

'Why didn't you send them out?'

Katie heard the surprise in Jack's voice.

'Send just the kids?' Peter replied, his voice quite clear above the increasing static of the radio. 'Can you imagine the trouble I had when I suggested it? We're in a small clinic plane, remember! With Janet on the stretcher, there would have been a seat for each of the kids and one seat left for one parent—and only one! The two families came close to fisticuffs on the verandah.'

'Grandparents, aunts and all?' Jack responded sympathetically, and Katie smiled. The 'family' groups of aboriginal people confused most outsiders, and their traditional support for each other in times of crisis could leave medical and hospital staff sighing in frustration.

'The lot! Anyway, they opted to keep the children here. I think the wind and the cyclone warning might have helped their decision—it's rough out there and the flight won't be much fun! Once the families decided the kids should stay, I decided to stay with them.'

Of course you would, Katie thought, understanding his decision but uneasy over the inherent dangers.

'I'll send the C200 tomorrow. You can bring them all out in that.'

'Thanks, Jack,' Peter said, his voice cutting in and out as the reception worsened. 'In the meantime, you might see if you can find someone who remembers an outbreak of a virus they thought might have been MVE back in the fifties. One of the local elders claims this is similar.'

Katie watched as Jack wrote 'MVE' and 'fifties' on one of the pads that littered the radio desk.

'I'll check it out,' he promised. 'You keep in touch.'

As Jack moved away, Katie took his place and spoke again.

'I'll stay on duty tonight, Peter,' she said. 'Call whenever you can and, remember, even if you can't hear us we shall probably be able to hear you. I can pass messages on the state emergency services if necessary.'

'You don't have to stay, Katie.' His voice lacked expression over the airwaves. 'I'll hit the call-up button if there's an emergency, and the answering service can contact you then.'

'I'll stay, Peter,' she said, and signed off before he could argue with her. The phone rang as she switched off the radio and she lifted the receiver, acknowledging that the greatest part of her work these days was answering telephones.

'Phone consultation, Jack,' she said, turning to where he was again swearing at a computer. 'It's Ellie Cross, out at Ruthven. One of the stockman has a high temperature and chills.'

As Jack responded to the call he waved a piece of paper at Katie. With one hand over the mouthpiece, he whispered, 'Could you tell Leonie about the cyclone warning for our area? She should send the clerical staff home and leave early herself to prepare—in case this is the one that doesn't veer away! Then look up MVE in our files; I think the letters stand for Murray Valley Virus—although that should be V, not E! Look for both. If we've struck it before there will be reference-book numbers for follow-up information.'

She left the radio room, and walked past the desks in the open office area. Christa Cassimatis, one of the flight sisters, was busy writing up case notes and Sally Hawker, the junior clerk, was handling some of the mountains of filing the base seemed to generate.

Katie crossed to the base manager's door, and knocked lightly on the outer wall to attract Leonie's attention.

'Jack asked me to let you know that the low in the Coral Sea has been upgraded to a cyclone and there's a warning current for this area. He thought you might like to send the staff home early.'

Leonie glanced at her watch, sighed, then frowned.

'Well, you might let the others know and tell them to go whenever they're ready. I'll finish up my work here, then head for home! You'll switch through to the answering service when you go?'

'I'm staying,' Katie announced, and watched the clear soft skin pucker between Leonie's eyebrows.

'Why, Katie? I know it's only a warning, but if the cyclone continues to move towards the coast flying debris will make driving too dangerous for you to leave much later.'

'Peter's at Coorawalla with no phone contact, and his cyclone is much closer than ours. I'll stay by the radio in case he needs to talk to us but don't worry, I won't be venturing outside. I'll let my parents know I'm here for the night.'

She passed on the message to the others, then returned to the radio room. Jack was still speaking to Ellie on a cattle property fifty minutes' flying time from Rainbow Bay. Katie listened to the calm repetition of his instructions as she began a search through their records. Although the Bay base had only been operating for fifteen years a précis of all existing medical records from other bases, beginning with the first established in Cloncurry in 1927, had been fed into the computer system.

She knew enough to be aware of the value of these records. Treatments might change almost daily, but human reaction to attack—whether physical or environmental—didn't, which meant that the signs and symptoms remained the same. A diagnosis of something rare could often be found by digging into the past.

MVE came up—Murray Valley Encephalitis—epidemic in the southern Australian area around the Murray River Valley, isolated and named in 1952. She read the effects of the virus with growing concern.

'Found anything?'

Jack turned from the phone and leaned across the table towards her. 'Yes,' she said, her eyes still on the computer screen. 'And none of it good! Spread by mosquitoes, thought to come from the northern areas of Australia but carried south occasionally by birds. No antibiotics or vaccine available, but if patients can be kept alive the disease will run its course.'

'You don't sound particularly cheerful about that aspect of it,' Jack said, and Katie shook her head.

'You'd understand the words better than I do, but it says here that it frequently affects the meninges and can cause neural damage. People badly affected may survive because of sophisticated life-support machines but they could suffer some degree of brain damage when they recover.'

'Book references?'

She gave him the reference numbers of the books listed on the screen and watched him cross to the library shelves.

'I'll read up on this MVE,' he told her, 'then talk to the hospital. Let me know when you get an ETA from Eddie. I'd like to go down and meet them. Janet's been a colleague since I started here at Rainbow Bay.'

He walked to the door, then turned back towards her.

'Are you happy to stay by the radio this evening? I could get one of the men to come in.'

'No way!' Katie said. Back in the days when the radio had been manned twenty-four hours a day most of the operators had been men. Occasionally, retired male operators were called in during emergencies which required a listener on hand. 'Do you really think that the first woman chief radio officer of Rainbow Bay is going to relinquish her responsibilities to a *man*?'

Jack smiled at her and walked away.

Not that chief radio officer was anything other than a courtesy title, she reminded herself. She closed the medical files on the computer and brought the duty rosters back onto the screen. These days phones had taken over most radio work, and commercial radio operators would soon provide listening posts for radio users.

Eventually the mighty link between radio and the Royal
Flying Doctor Service would be severed for the first
time since a clever engineer called Alf Traegar joined
John Flynn in his endeavours to give the lonely outback
a voice.

Eddie's call to tell her their arrival time at the Bay
reminded her that some radio messages would still have
a place in their system.

'You'll have heard a cyclone warning's been issued
here now?' Katie checked.

'Caught it on the weather band. Would you mind
phoning my home and telling our boys to stay put?'
Eddie asked, adding, 'That's if they've gone home.
Heaven knows what trouble those two could get into if
left to their own devices during a cyclone alert!'

'I'll track them down,' she promised, and signed off.

She switched to the local radio channel to monitor
the alerts which would come through with increasing
frequency while the second cyclone continued to head
towards the coast, and tried the Stones' house to see if
their teenage twins had arrived home. She let the phone
ring while she fielded another radio call.

'Eddie again, Katie. The control tower at the Bay
doesn't want us coming in there. The weather bureau
has them right on track for the cyclone and they don't
want to risk cluttering up the airstrip with the wrecks
of crashed light planes which tried to land in the
strengthening winds.'

'What will you do?' she asked, knowing that he could
choose to go north-east to Wyrangi or south to one of
the bigger towns out of their area.

'I'll head for Mt Isa,' he said. 'There's a good hospital
there for Janet and we'll be handy enough to fly back to
Coorawalla or the Bay tomorrow, depending on where
we're needed in the clean-up operations. Tell them

we'll be there by six. Did you find the boys?'

'Not yet, but I will,' Katie promised. 'I'll let Mt Isa hospital know about Janet and arrange for an ambulance to meet you at the airport. Jack's here. He was going to go and meet the plane, but now he can find the twins and take care of them instead.'

She switched channels again, and hung up the unanswered phone. Typical afternoon, she thought, with a couple of cyclones thrown in for variety! She scanned the airwaves for calls, alert for any emergency as the weather deteriorated on both sides of the cape.

'Call the Centre for Tropical Medicine at James Cook University, would you, please, Katie, and get them to fax through any up-to-date information they have on MVE? When you get something send a copy to Dr Allan at the hospital, and if you're talking to Peter give him any treatment details that might be helpful.'

Jack had whirled into the room to stand beside her, while the Klaxons heralded the latest warning.

'Still coming this way and picking up strength,' Jack muttered, summarising the information succinctly.

'I thought it must be,' Katie told him. 'Eddie radioed to say they're diverting to Mt Isa. Do you want to talk to the hospital there about Janet and fax any information to them instead?'

'I'll talk to them,' he said. 'It will give me something to do. You can send on information later.'

Katie could see the impatience that strained at him. He would have preferred to be at Coorawalla in Peter's place, or caring for Janet on the plane.

'There'll be plenty for you to do later if this cyclone hits,' she reminded him. 'And I've a job for you now—as soon as you've phoned the hospital.'

She explained Eddie's concern.

'If you could find the twins and arrange for them

either to stay with you or go to Leonie's place and then let Eddie and Susan know, it would be a great help. Susan's got her mobile, and if they keep ringing and getting an empty house they'll go mad with worry.'

'So I'm the babysitter now?' he said, and she smiled at him.

'Unless you'd rather be the radio operator?'

That won an answering smile. Out beyond the ranges, children of four could tune in to their pre-school sessions from the School of Distance Education on the radio, but put Jack anywhere near it. . .

He disappeared towards his office, returning half an hour later.

'I'm off to find those boys,' he told her. 'If they're not at home I'll leave a note to say I'm looking for them and to stay put until I contact them. If, by some odd chance, they ring in to enquire about their parents' whereabouts, tell them the same thing. Are you sure you'll be OK on your own here? I could bring them back here and we could all sit out the night together.'

'I'll be fine,' Katie told him. 'I grew up in this town, remember. I'm a cyclone survivor from way back! If you're looking for togetherness, you could check on Allysha. Nick's in Wyrangi so she'll be on her own, and this will be her first experience of a bit of a blow.'

'Bit of a blow! I like that,' he said, smiling at her matter-of-fact acceptance of the situation. 'I'll find Allysha as well. If Nick contacts you, reassure him that she's safe! I've left the vents open at the back of the building, Katie,' he added and she nodded, knowing the strange-looking metal shutters he was talking about. They had been installed when the old house that was the base office had been made 'cyclone-proof' some years earlier, and provided an escape route for the wind if front doors or windows were blown in.

'There's still plenty of time for it to veer away from us,' she reminded him. 'We must get a dozen warnings a season, but it's been four years since a cyclone crossed the coast and that was hundreds of kilometres south of the Bay. It could easily be a false alarm!'

'I hope you're right,' Jack said, and hurried away.

'Ambulance!' Katie muttered to herself. 'Then the university and try the Stones' again.'

She made the call to Mt Isa, then tried to raise Peter at Coorawalla to check on the situation there.

No answer!

But that could be because he was busy moving patients, drugs and dressings into the safe central core, she told herself.

Another consultation call came through from one of the station properties they serviced, the caller oblivious of the natural dramas occurring on two distant boundaries of their base area. She switched the caller through to Jack's mobile and rang the university.

The university research librarian promised to fax any information they had on MVE as quickly as possible, and Peter radioed to say that his patients were all secure in the 'safe cell' of the hospital building.

'The winds are raging outside,' he said. 'It's like a world gone mad. Can you hear the thuds and thumps as branches are thrown against the building?'

Katie shook her head. She could hear static and more static, with Peter's voice barely audible through the interference.

'I'm waiting on more information on MVE to come through from the university,' she told him. 'Eddie's diverted to Mt Isa and Janet will be transferred to hospital there. Jack's spoken to the hospital and passed on your suspicions. He's worried sick about you, so keep your head down.'

Who's worried sick about him? she asked herself, one hand pressed against her churning stomach. Then she forgot her own discomfort as the crackling suggested that Peter was speaking again.

'I'll call hourly, Katie.'

She made out the words with difficulty.

'I'll be here,' she promised.

Then, for some strange reason, the phones stopped ringing and she no longer had the excuse of being busy to stop the worry that ate at her mind. She phoned her parents, explaining that she wouldn't be home until morning and assuring them she wouldn't leave the building until the radio gave an all-clear.

The fax came through from the university and, when a change in the static told her an hour later that Peter was radioing in, she read out the information but heard no acknowledgement that he'd received it.

Not that it would have helped him much. It offered more details on the spread of the disease than its treatment.

Another hour dragged by and she fiddled with the dials, praying that she would hear his voice this time.

'. . .quiet. . .unearthly. . .passing over. . . Are you there, Katie?'

'I'm here, Peter,' she said, licking her lips to ease the dryness. 'I'll be here all night.'

And as she made the pledge she knew that, if he had heard it, he would smile and think, Good old Katie! He would see it as a sign of her devotion to duty—this all-night stint at the radio when a second cyclone was approaching the Bay.

But he didn't know about the other cyclone, she reminded herself.

And he certainly didn't—and wouldn't—know that her 'devotion' might be to him, not duty! That was something he would never know!

She sighed.

'That was a big sigh, Katie.'

The voice made her spin around—grateful she hadn't been speaking her thoughts aloud in what she'd imagined was an empty building.

'Allysha! What on earth are you doing here? Haven't you heard the cyclone warning? Isn't it blowing outside?'

She looked at the young woman, who was still recovering from burns received on an evacuation flight. There was a patch of shiny redness on her forehead and her eyelids were still too bright a pink, but the happiness which shone in her eyes and danced in every step she took minimised the impact of the scars and made it impossible not to smile in response to her ebullient joy.

'It's blowing like hell,' she confirmed, 'but I did my last practice flight earlier today. One hundred miserable hours I've had to put in before that wretched Eddie would let me back up in one of our planes! I kept telling him I'd have crashed the first time if I couldn't see properly but, no, I had to go right back to basics and do my time all over again.'

Her slight figure had stiffened with disgust, but the nimbus of love that seemed to hover around her softened the impact of her outrage.

'As soon as I landed from that last flight I decided I'd complete the logbook and bring it over here. I'll leave it on Eddie's desk. He won't keep me out of the air now, will he?'

Katie heard the uncertainty behind Allysha's bravado.

'Of course, he won't,' she said quickly. 'He'll be delighted to have you back on the roster. He hasn't stopped complaining about losing his best pilot since it happened.'

Allysha blushed at the compliment.

'I'd better leave these and be off,' she said quickly, as if to cover her reaction, then she looked around and frowned. 'Why are you here all alone if there's a cyclone coming?'

'Peter's at Coorawalla and they're having their own cyclone problems!' Katie told her. 'His only link is the radio so I'm staying on in case he calls.'

'But Coorawalla's in the gulf. Nick's at Wyrangi!'

Katie heard the beginning of panic in her voice.

'You're a pilot!' she chided gently. 'You should know Wyrangi's as far from Coorawalla as we are. Who's flying Nick?'

'Michael Ward,' Allysha answered, visibly relieved by Katie's calming words. 'His wife's mother is staying with them for a while, freeing Michael to go back on his old clinic run.' She paused before continuing, 'But this will be his last. I'll be on the next one!'

The determination in her voice made Katie smile. Allysha's and Nick's love had become apparent to everyone who had visited her in hospital, where Nick had sat by her bed whenever he wasn't working—calming her fears and making light of the possibility of blindness.

'Will you finally give in and marry poor Nick once you've flown another clinic run?' Katie asked, and saw her answer in the smile that lit up Allysha's face.

'Of course I will,' she said. 'We've already wasted too much time.'

She hesitated, then added, 'But I couldn't marry him knowing I might not get my sight back. I couldn't have saddled him with such a dependent wife!'

'Nick wouldn't have cared,' Katie said, remembering

her own envy when she'd seen the way Nick had looked at his injured love.

'But I would have,' Allysha said quietly.

The radio stuttered back to life, interrupting them, but it was impossible to pick up any distinguishable words.

'I'll leave this and get going—unless you'd like me to stay,' Allysha said. 'Would you like some company?'

Katie shook her head, only half-aware of Allysha's presence as she manipulated the dials in an effort to find clearer transmission.

'You get home,' she said. 'Once Nick hears there's a warning out for Rainbow Bay he'll be trying to reach you, and Jack's going to be checking on you as well. He's in charge of the ''Base family'' —deserted wives, sweethearts and children!'

She leaned towards the speaker, trying to distinguish human sounds in the scratchy, spluttering noise.

'Well, good luck,' Allysha said. Katie heard her footsteps echo through the empty building, then the slamming of a door told her that she was alone again.

The interference failed to reveal a voice, although her fingers shook with the effort of trying to find one.

Silence settled around her, but when she walked through to the kitchen to fill the insulated jug with coffee and get a sandwich she realised how bad the weather was getting at the Bay. Trees in the tropical base gardens tossed and bent double before the wind in the early dusk, and rain threw itself in horizontal sheets across the windows. She shivered at the evidence of the power which nature could unleash.

Carrying the coffee and her snack, she returned to the soundproofed radio room—pleased to be snugly warm and dry inside.

'Can you hear me, Katie?'

Definitely Peter! Relief washed over her. The eye of

the cyclone would have been over Coorawalla when he'd spoken of the unearthly stillness. It would have been followed by more fierce and destructive winds as the ferocity of nature's might continued on its path. Yet Peter was still alive.

The thoughts flashed through her head, while her lips repeated again and again, 'I can hear you, Peter, go ahead.'

For a long time there was only more static, then his voice came faltering through.

'We're all OK here,' he said, 'but trapped at the moment.'

'So much for cyclone-proof buildings,' she muttered fiercely to herself.

'Something must have blown across the hospital, and one wall has caved in. I repeat, we are all OK. Can you hear me, Katie?'

Her heart stuttered for a moment, but she spoke her assurances calmly.

'I have your message that you're all OK, Peter,' she said. 'Keep talking; I can hear you quite clearly now.'

But could he hear her? The base receiver was more powerful than the radio he had in his 'safe cell' at the hospital.

'The boys both slept through it, and the other patient is fine. By the sound of things the wind is still blowing strongly outside. It could be morning before anyone is able to get to us.'

Get to us? Is that what he'd said or had the crackling distorted his words.

'Just how trapped are you, Peter?' she asked, trying to halt the panicky acceleration of her heartbeats.

Static filled the silence, then his voice came through again.

'Pretty trapped! I think the drug-cabinet fell across

my legs but, as I'm face down, I can't turn around to look. The patients were on the floor—on mattresses under their bed-frames. I can reach out and touch all of them, so I know they're OK.'

Vivid images of the chaos blurred Katie's concentration on the radio dials.

'You said a wall came down, Peter,' she said, hoping that her apprehension wasn't transferring itself through the airwaves. 'Where's the wall, and what's supporting the ceiling and roof?'

More screeching interference, but she managed to pick up the words,

'. . .wall on top of bed-frames; imagine the roof's on top of that again. It must be somewhere,' she heard him add with something of his natural humour, 'because we're not getting wet.'

'Well, be thankful for small mercies,' she replied tartly as her concern verged towards anger.

'Talk to me, Katie!' he said, but was the reception weaker or was it his voice losing strength?

She responded to the plea, and began talking.

CHAPTER TWO

AT TIMES, during that long night, Katie was aware of the wildness beyond the building. At times she shivered when the howling of gale-force winds echoed eerily through the empty rooms of the building. She wondered if Peter was still there—if he could hear her talking—if he was still alive.

The timbers of the old house moaned their protest at the wind, and for a moment she thought that perhaps she had made the noise.

'He's trapped, not badly hurt,' she reminded herself, speaking the words aloud to chase unwelcome ghosts of 'maybes' away. 'Think of practical things, Katie!' she admonished.

Was his radio still working?

She kept talking while her thoughts chased down random paths, wayward as rabbits. Surely, with their powerful receiver, she should be able to hear him? Because of their sensitive radio system the base had a generator which cut in if the city's electricity was lost, but Peter would be relying on batteries. Were his batteries flat?

Was the drug-cabinet heavy? Could the roof cave in on a building designed and built to cyclone standards?

Was static cutting out her words? It was certainly all she could hear!

But he had asked her to talk to him, and she talked. At first about the base and what was happening here, then about the staff and, finally—when all other words evaded her—she talked about herself, telling him things about her past; about growing up as the only child of older parents; about being a child whose father was a minister in a town where religion was not a popular commodity.

As a change in the quality of the light told her that the night was ending she listened again, hoping for some acknowledgement from Peter and praying that she would pick up something other than the crackling interference she'd been hearing since his last transmission nine hours earlier.

She twirled the dial through the bands, although she knew exactly where she'd pick up his voice if it came through again. The phone rang as she came back to that point but when she reached out and lifted the receiver it was dead.

The ringing continued and she swung around in her seat, finally locating a mobile phone which had been left on the table behind her.

'Are you OK, Katie?' Jack's voice asked.

'I'm fine! Why?' she asked, her sleep-deprived brain puzzled by the concern in his voice.

'Because the town's been blown about by a category two cyclone, that's why,' he said sharply. 'Don't tell me you didn't even notice it over there? They can't have strengthened the building that much.'

Category two—not too bad: minor damage to houses; significant damage to trees, she thought, remembering words she'd learnt in her radio operator's course.

'I did hear it blowing, but I'm quite safe. I've been in the radio room all night,' she said, hoping that would be an acceptable explanation. In fact, her concentration had been so focussed on Peter at Coorawalla that she'd only occasionally been aware of what was happening in her immediate surroundings.

'How's Peter?'

Jack would ask!

'I had the channel open and have been talking to him, but I haven't heard anything for some time,' she told him, keeping her voice steady with an enormous effort. She didn't add, he's trapped. There was no point in two of them worrying themselves sick.

'I'll get over there as soon as I can, and I'll find someone to relieve you. Until then, keep trying for a response.'

She nodded. Someone who was more awake than she was would have to man the radio this morning. While mopping-up operations began here in Rainbow Bay the calls for medical help from neighbouring areas would begin to filter in. Once it was safe for people to venture out of their houses the first priority would be communication.

Her fingers faltered on the channel-finder. Surely she would hear from Peter before she was forced to go off duty?

'Katie?'

His voice came through the static as if he had heard her thoughts and she felt the tears of relief sliding down her cheeks, hot against her cold skin.

'I'm here, Peter. Are you OK?'

The words were almost strangled as they squeezed past the lump in her throat.

'You stopped talking,' he accused, then any further words were lost as the reception faded again.

She put her head down on her hands and closed her eyes, letting the relief wash over her.

'Can you hear me, base?'

Training reasserted itself and she acknowledged the new radio call, reaching for the mobile phone with one hand to silence the second summons.

It was the beginning of the most hectic hour of her

life and even when Jack arrived with Ken Williams, an
experienced radio operator, she was still unable to leave
because the phone lines had been restored in their area
and phone consultations were coming in faster than she
could field them.

'Come on, I'll drive you home, Katie. Sally's here.
She can handle the phone until I get back.'

She looked up to see Leonie in the doorway of the
radio room, and smiled weakly.

'I can drive,' she protested but, as she stood and felt
the weakness in her knees, she decided that it would
be nice to be driven.

Outside the building neighbours worked to clear
broken branches and uprooted trees. Katie shook her
head in wonder that all this destruction could have happened while she sat snugly in the radio room, talking
the night away.

'It's a good thing there are no trees near the car park
or you'd have had branches and dents for decoration,'
Leonie said, waving her hand to where Katie's car
stood, disguised by a mantle of leaves.

'I'm glad I don't have to clean it up right now,'
Katie admitted, as tiredness hit her with the force of a
sledgehammer. She slid thankfully into the passenger
seat of Leonie's car, and leant back against the head-
rest. Leonie had turned to speak to someone who was
calling from the building, but she couldn't hear the
conversation.

'Ken had a message for you from Peter,' Leonie told
her as they drove off.

'Message from Peter?' Katie echoed fuzzily.

'Message from Peter,' Leonie reiterated, and it
sounded to Katie's exhausted mind as if she was smiling
inside when she said it.

'He said, first free night he has he'll buy you dinner!'

Tired as she was, she felt a flush of heat start at her toes and work its way up her body. She pushed herself self-consciously back into the seat, hoping that her embarrassment wasn't showing as a bright red blush on her cheeks. Red cheeks and hazel eyes would look peculiar, she was certain.

She glanced at Leonie, who was driving through the litter of rubbish on the streets with a frown of concentration on her face. She couldn't have thought anything of the invitation—or seen the blush, if it had shown!

Katie sighed inwardly. She knew that Peter had only asked out of kindness and she probably wouldn't go with him anyway, but she wouldn't want anyone at the base thinking that she. . .

Was one of Peter's women?

The uncharitable thought hammered in her head and she lifted a hand and ran it through her hair, hoping that the movement might clear her clogged-up thought processes.

'Here you are!' Leonie stopped outside the low-set house which had been Katie's home since childhood.

'Thanks, Leonie,' she said, climbing a little unsteadily out of the car. She looked around at the tattered remnants of the garden and sighed. Her mother, a devoted gardener, would be there somewhere, cutting back the damaged limbs of trees and talking consolingly to her plants, while her father would be out helping in the general clean-up.

'Go and get some sleep,' Leonie ordered, waving her away from the car. 'And don't say no to Peter when he asks you properly.'

The car moved off before Katie could reply, and she stood and watched it disappear down the road.

He won't ask me properly, she told herself and, turning towards the house, she called to her mother, then

set off in the direction of the answering yell. One quick
good morning, then she could go to bed! Sleep should
banish futile thoughts of Peter.

Peter had known that his ankle was injured long before
the rescuers lifted the roof, and then the wall and finally
the drug-cabinet off it. All through the night it had
throbbed with such painful persistence that sleep had
been nothing more than a few swift snatches of oblivion.

And through it all Katie had talked to him, her
voice flickering in the interference, hesitant at times
and fading to nothing at others, yet like a lifeline to
normality—to a world that hadn't been blown apart by
a primeval fury.

He had even pictured her, hunched forward a little
at the radio desk, her wide hazel eyes intent on the dials
and her hair falling forward like thick curtains around
her face. He realised, as he listened, that physically she
hid behind her hair, swinging it forward to shield her
face. Did she hide her emotions in the same way?
Behind her quiet, matter-of-fact manner and sensible,
work-orientated conversation? Or was what you saw
what you got with Katie?

He'd never given her much thought, except as a fellow employee at the base—and an efficient one at that!
But as she'd talked through the night, revealing facets
of a person he had never dreamed existed, he'd become
intrigued and his image of her had altered slightly,
coming into a clearer focus—as if a gauzy curtain had
been drawn aside. He smiled to himself as he looked
around the shattered building.

'Are you there, Peter? This is Jack. Please acknowledge if you can hear me.'

'Radio wants you, Doc.'

One of his rescuers passed the mike towards him,

trailing the cord across the two young patients, to where he sat, propped against the one remaining wall in a small space now cleared of debris.

'I can hear you, Jack,' he said, then clicked to receive.

'How are things there? Disaster Relief has asked us to send the C200, but when I spoke to their headquarters on the island I was told they hadn't found you. Something about the hospital being among the worst affected buildings.'

Tired as he was, Peter felt another smile stretch his lips. Jack would deny it if he was accused of fussing, but he did take his responsibility for his staff seriously.

'They've found me now,' he told Jack, 'and my patients. We're all present and correct. The two boys are still very sick and I'd like them lifted out as soon as possible. As well as the boys, I've two badly injured women. One received a deep gash on the upper arm and lost too much blood for me to replace solely with fluids and the other, I suspect, has a fractured pelvis.

'At the moment the hospital is a concrete floor, a pile of rubbish pushed to one side as a windbreak and a big tarpaulin that's keeping off most of the rain. If anyone else with serious injuries is brought in they'll also have to be taken somewhere else until the building is restored.'

'The air force is flying an army relief crew in,' Jack told him. 'They could bring people out if you need more transport. Now, are you OK to cope medically if I send a nurse but no doctor on the big plane? That way, I can bring Eddie back here so there's a plane and a doctor available for other evacuation flights.'

'I'll cope,' Peter said and signed off. He glanced down at his swollen ankle and the crutches which lay beside him on the floor. Jack had sounded worried enough without knowing about that! It was only ligament damage, he was sure. Ice would help but, as the island had had no power for fourteen hours, ice wasn't an option.

He levered himself to his feet, and hitched the crutches under his armpits. At least he had them to help him move about. They had been left on the hospital verandah the previous day, and had somehow survived undamaged. His ankle throbbed. Would another two painkillers make him a drug addict? He had to get outside to see if the men sifting through the ruins of the hospital had found a stretcher.

'Store cupboard all stove in, Doc,' one of the helpers told him cheerfully.

'Keep digging,' he told the man. 'Apart from anything else, the community can't afford to have to replace all the equipment that's in there.'

He frowned at the new complication, and swung himself gingerly across the wet, rubbish-littered floor to where an elderly woman rested uneasily on an old door which had been used to transport her to the hospital.

'Hang in there, Ruby,' he said, pressing the woman's hand gently. 'There's a beautiful pressure mattress on the plane, especially for you.'

His fingers shifted to her wrist and he felt the rapid pulse that told him she was still suffering, in spite of a painkilling injection only an hour earlier.

The co-ordinator of the disaster relief committee arrived as he was examining the younger of the two boys.

'Who are you taking on your plane?' he asked Peter. 'We're going to have to airlift half the community off the island until we get water and power back on,' he explained, without waiting for a reply. 'If I send the relatives of your passengers on the first air force flight you won't have to worry about their transport.'

Peter nodded his agreement. The disaster relief committees in isolated areas might meet for years without ever having to put their theories into practice, but he was impressed by what he had seen of the clean-up operation at Coorawalla.

'Were there no other injuries? No deaths?' Peter asked, amazed that a wind strong enough to destroy what was supposed to be a 'cyclone-proof' building had not done more damage to the humans on the island.

'Old Lydia died,' the man said, tears welling in his dark eyes. 'She told us, when she came back to Coorawalla from that hospital on the mainland, that she was waiting for a big wind to take her spirit.'

'Some big wind!' Peter said, shaking his head and smiling at the description. 'She must have had a mighty spirit.'

He didn't ask to see the body, nor did he need to certify her death. Lydia had tried white man's medicine when she'd first been diagnosed with cancer, then had chosen to return to her home and wait for the end in her own way and among her own people. It was fitting that the tribal elders performed the rites of death for Lydia.

'I'll send a truck to take your patients to the airport as soon as we get an ETA on the plane,' the co-ordinator promised, then he left to organise the evacuation of elderly people, women and children from the island while Peter turned his attention to his patients.

'Can't do much for these kids?' the aide asked.

'We can treat the symptoms, that's all,' he said quietly. Once they reached hospital a lumbar puncture could withdraw a little cerebro-spinal fluid for testing. Instinct told him that the lab would find traces of the MVE virus and, if that was the case, the effort involved in the clean-up operations after Willie would be nothing compared to the scientific search for antibodies and carriers which would follow news of the outbreak.

Excitement surfaced through the nagging pain, and he hoped that the research team would be based at the Bay so that he could stay involved.

'Radio says plane due in soon,' the aide called.

He forgot about MVE and hobbled over to where the workers were shifting timber and wall panels off what had been the store-room.

'Come on, you guys,' he encouraged, using one crutch to flick a splintered piece of wood aside. 'I'd like to know what's usable in there before I leave. I can replace some of the equipment with gear from the plane so you've got splints and stretchers for emergencies.'

'Not much that's good still in there, I guess,' one of the workers told him. 'See that tree.'

He pointed to a pile of branches, stripped of leaves, and what had been a massive tree-trunk, now sawn into five fat logs.

'He came down on the store-room,' the man explained. 'Pushed that cyclone wall over and brought the roof down.'

'So the building didn't blow in like a house of straw,' Peter said. 'I don't know if that makes me feel better or worse. I suppose the lesson is not to build cyclone-proof buildings too close to massive great trees!'

The men smiled, and bent again to their work. Knowing that there was nothing he could do to help, he went back and checked the contents of the battered drug-cabinet. He could replenish that from the plane stock also. All the inhabitants of the island community had been accounted for, with miraculously few injuries, but the clean-up operations would bring their own rash of minor concerns as workers happened upon angry snakes or brushed their skin against razor-sharp pieces of corrugated iron.

'Truck here, Doc,' the aide called, and he looked out to see a man in army fatigues approaching.

'You fellows got here quickly,' he said, offering his hand to the man.

'Beat your plane in by a few minutes,' the man said. 'Have you any priorities we should know about? Any particular risk of disease, for instance?'

'How many men have you brought in?' Peter asked, as the possibility of an MVE epidemic rang in his head.

'Forty, counting the doctor and nurse. They are both at the airfield, checking out your new plane, but they'll stay on here. There's always someone getting hurt in these operations.'

'Do they have their own drugs and equipment?' Peter asked, and was relieved to see an answering nod. That saved him one worry. 'Are you in charge?'

The man nodded again, and Peter called to the men working on the store-room.

'Would you fellows help carry the patients to the truck?' he asked, and waved to the aide to organise them. Then he turned back to the newcomer.

'I'd like you to come back out to the airport with me. I need to talk to you and the medical people. There might be a bigger problem here than you think.'

He manoeuvred his body around so that he could watch the patients being loaded.

'Leave Ruby,' he said. 'I'll send the pressure mattress back for her. The flight sister will tell you what to do when you lift her onto it.'

As the two boys, the woman with the injured arm and an elderly, bedridden man were settled in the covered truck, he followed and heaved himself into the cabin. The army officer clambered in the back, and they set off through piles of rubbish towards the airstrip.

'The last time one of these outbreaks occurred,' he explained a little later to the grave-faced military personnel, 'researchers took blood from everything they could find—humans, domestic fowls and animals, and native birds and animals. They found antibodies of the virus in every species, including the humans, yet some of the people who had antibodies had never been sick.'

'So the animals and birds have an immunity to it, and it obviously doesn't affect the mosquitoes who carry it. Is there a possibility that the local people may be developing a similar immunity?' the doctor asked.

'Yes, some of them must be if you consider the antibodies. But the emphasis is on "the local people",' Peter confirmed. 'You've got forty newcomers here, all of whom have every chance of being bitten by mosquitoes and none of whom will have any immunity.'

He saw the impact of his words in their faces.

'Back in the war years, when the army was trying to stop the spread of malaria among the troops in New Guinea, they poured kerosene on every waterhole in the vicinity of the camp to kill the mosquito larvae,' the doctor said, and Peter looked at him in horror.

'This area is renowned for its bird life,' he stuttered. 'You can't do that!'

The man smiled at him.

'No, but we've sprays that we can use to control the mosquitoes, which won't harm the wildlife or the environment, and, now you've made us aware of the problem, we can make certain every member of our group uses lashings of repellent and keeps covered up as much as possible.'

Peter nodded. It was the best he could do. The truck returned. Christa was squatting beside the woman on the pressure mattress which, once she was in position and the air suctioned out, fitted the patient like a body splint and prevented any movement.

Suddenly Peter felt the exhaustion which the need for action had kept at bay. He waited until this final passenger was loaded and then, using the crutches, he hefted his body up the steps and into the plane.

'Take me home, Bill,' he said to the pilot and sank down into a seat, doing up his seat belt automatically before closing his eyes and dropping into a dreamless sleep.

He woke as the plane touched down, but was relieved when Christa said, 'I've updated the file notes on all your patients for the hospital, and I'll see to the ambulance transfer. You should go with them and get your ankle X-rayed.'

'Thanks for doing the charts,' he said, relieved that the job he should have done had been completed while he slept. 'But I won't go with them. I'll go to one of the private radiology clinics,' he told her. 'My car's an automatic. I'll be able to drive.'

'You'll drive nowhere,' she said crossly as they taxied to a halt outside their hangar. 'Jack's meeting the plane. If you don't want to go up to the hospital, he'll take you to a clinic.'

She unlocked the door and activated the mechanism that would lower it and, with the steps barely touching the ground, Jack bounded into the cabin.

He looked first at each patient, touching and reassuring them as he asked how they were feeling. Peter saw him frown at the lassitude of the two boys, then the frown deepened when his eyes lit on the crutches propped beside his colleague.

'Minor ankle sprain,' Peter assured him, hiding the fact that his body felt as if it had been drawn through a mangle.

'I knew you were keeping something back,' Jack muttered at him. 'Come on, let's get you out of here.'

Peter held up his hand.

'Not so fast,' he said. 'Let's get the plane unloaded, then we'll talk. If I'm right and there's a live virus spreading through Coorawalla you're going to have more to do with your time than worry about me.'

Jack turned to watch the patients being helped or carried off the plane.

'You're talking about this MVE?' he asked when they were finally on their own.

Peter nodded.

'Did you have time to read the material the university faxed to the base?'

Jack looked surprised that he would know of it and Peter added, 'Katie read it out to me over the radio.'

'It's on my desk, but I haven't had time to look at it,' Jack told him.

Peter sighed.

'I've worried about it most of the night,' Peter explained, not adding, when I wasn't being soothed to sleep by some of Katie's stories. An image of Katie's hazel eyes flashed across his mind and he blinked it away, surprised by the intrusion and the strange comfort that accompanied it. 'Last time there was an outbreak a team from a southern university worked in the affected area for three months. They were the first people to isolate the live virus in a mosquito, but they didn't find the host animal or bird.'

'And did they find an effective cure? What was the prognosis?'

'There's no effective cure or treatment, apart from keeping the patient alive.' Peter paused before he added the really bad news. 'During the first outbreak there was a sixty per cent mortality rate.'

'Sixty per cent! Two of those three patients we've seen already could die?'

'Not these days, with life support,' Peter told him, 'but as the illness runs its course it destroys brain cells so rapidly that the risk of permanent brain damage escalates. If you take the problem a step further, you're looking at a small, largely self-sufficient community like Coorawalla faced with the problems of providing for a disproportionate number of people with intellectual and physical disabilities.'

'A community under our mantle,' Jack said softly, and Peter knew that he was thinking of the physical and mental strain this would place on families. 'So we've got to try to control it—to prevent its spread. The university will help with researchers. Did you explain this to the relief team that's flown up there today?'

Peter nodded and smiled. Jack had completely forgotten the injured ankle in his desire to get on with combating the potentially deadly virus. He muttered something about the hospital and hurried away.

'I haven't forgotten you're injured,' Christa said as she bundled dirty linen into a bag for the laundry. 'I'll drive you back to the base and someone there can take you for an X-ray.'

'OK, bossy one!' Peter said, giving in gracefully as the lethargy of tiredness swept over him again. He checked his watch—ten minutes to two! If he remembered his roster correctly he was on call for another thirty hours. He hoped that no one would need him for the next five or six of them. He had to get some sleep.

Katie looked down at Peter's sun-streaked golden thatch of hair and his smooth, honey-coloured skin. He was

definitely the best-looking man she had ever seen, even
with his blue eyes closed and a rash of dark stubble
across his cheeks and chin.

Someone had thrown a blanket over him, but a ban-
daged foot stuck out at the end of the uncomfortable
bed that was pushed up against the wall of the radio
room. It had been left there from the days when radio
officers slept over, waiting for calls which might never
come. Now it remained so that tired flight staff could
snatch some sleep between evacuation flights if they
didn't feel like making the journey to their homes.

She glanced at her watch. Six o'clock!

Having caught up on her own lost sleep, she had
walked back to the base to clean the leaves from her
car and drive it home. A light inside the building had
drawn her in, and the sleeping man now held all her
attention.

He stirred as she watched and she stepped backwards,
not wanting to be caught hovering over him. Her heel
clipped the metal waste-paper basket which clanged into
a table leg before scattering its contents over the floor.

Heart thumping, she knelt to collect the papers, shov-
ing them back into the tin. Then she lifted her head—
warily—as fearful as if she'd been guilty of an indecent
act of voyeurism.

Peter's blue eyes were open, and she rather thought
they might be twinkling at her.

'My guardian angel!' he said sleepily, and held out
his hand.

The table prevented her backing even further away,
and the sight of those long, strong fingers and broad
palm extended towards her gave her the kind of palpi-
tations patients often described over the radio or phone.

'You look like a frightened rabbit about to disappear
into its burrow, crouching there under the table,' he

teased, and she prayed for the floor to open just enough for her to sink through into a kindly oblivion.

'I knocked over the paper bin,' she said weakly, her head bent so that her hair would hide her embarrassment.

'And is it a penance for your clumsiness that you're going to stay in that uncomfortable position under the table? Do get up, Katie!' he urged. 'I'm sure it's straining my neck looking at you, and it's definitely making my ankle ache more.'

'Nonsense!' she stammered, easing herself out from under the table but avoiding the hand which remained stretched out from the bed. 'What happened to your ankle?' she asked, desperate to find a safe topic of conversation. 'Did you hurt it when the drug-cabinet fell?'

'The drug-cabinet, the wall and the roof,' he reminded her. 'Now, are you going to take my hand or is it going to flop out there like a stranded jellyfish all evening?'

'Why would I take your hand?' she quavered through breath that fluttered unevenly in her throat.

'So I can draw you over near the bed, look into your eyes and say thank you, Katie!'

She shrank back further.

'I won't bite, you know,' he added. 'And holding my hand won't contaminate you.'

She took a tentative step towards him, determined to get the conversation back on sensible ground.

'You don't have to thank me for anything,' she said. 'You were doing your job and I was doing my job. It was as simple as that!'

'Was it, Katie?' he said, and something in his voice made her look into his eyes. He shook his head, and the hand she'd refused to take moved to rest gently against her leg. 'To me, sharing something of your life with another person goes beyond duty.'

His gaze held hers as if he was trying to emphasise what he was saying, and his blue eyes seemed to be studying her intently. She tried to think what she'd said during that long night—how much she'd told him of her childhood, growing up as the child of a minister in a town that took religion lightly. And had she talked about her shyness? To this man who probably didn't know the meaning of the word?

'And that's what I want to thank you for!' he said, bringing her back to the present.

His hand rubbed up and down her calf, the touch electrifying her nerve-endings and sending her already overburdened heart into a frenzy.

'You—you must be hungry!' she stuttered. 'I'll get you something to eat and drink.'

She broke away—from the spell of his eyes and the magnetism of his touch—and dashed through to the kitchen-cum-lunchroom, where she slumped against the bench, pressed her hands to her chest and gave herself a stern lecture on control, and Peter's reputation, and reading things that didn't exist into simple gestures, and Peter's reputation, and the folly of unrequited love, and Peter's reputation, and. . .

CHAPTER THREE

STAFF meetings were held fortnightly, and as Katie carried extra chairs into the radio room she avoided looking at the bed which still had Peter's image imprinted on it in her mind.

'I hate Mondays,' Sally told her, dropping another chair into place around the big table that dominated the room.

Katie ignored the remark. On alternate Mondays, when there were no scheduled clinic flights, all employees not out of town on an evac flight or off duty were required to come to the base. These meetings were, to her, part of the essence of the Flying Doctors. Clerical staff, radio operators, pilots, doctors and nurses—all working together to provide a service for people in isolated places.

'It's all right for you,' Sally continued. 'You're older and you usually know what they're talking about and you can join in, but all I do is sit there and take notes.'

'I sat there and took notes for my first three or four years,' Katie reminded her, but she was pleased when Sally left the room to get the coffee-mugs. She would sneak a quick look at the bed and remember Peter holding out his hand to her.

'Good morning, Katie!'

She spun around, colouring guiltily.

'Good morning, Peter. How's your ankle?' She listened to the words come out and groaned inwardly at her predictable conversational opening! Why couldn't she scintillate?

42

'Still on three legs, Peter?' That was Allysha coming in—and scintillating quite brightly! A transparent joy bubbled from her skin and confidence rang in her voice. And why wouldn't she be confident and bubbly with Nick hovering like a guardian angel right behind her?

The greetings continued, and Katie slipped into her own chair, closer to her desk than to the table—ostensibly so that she could reach for the radio or phone but, in fact, because she felt more comfortable there—a little apart from the others. She sat back, happy in her role as listener and observer.

Eddie began the proceedings by saying how pleased he was to have Allysha flying again, and handing the next fortnight's pilot rosters to Leonie. Susan, as senior flight sister, came next.

'I've been thinking about Coorawalla,' she said. 'Peter's diagnosis of MVE was confirmed by tests, and Janet's not going to be well enough to return to work for some months.'

An unspoken 'if she's ever well enough' drifted through the air.

'The hospital will be rebuilt—thanks to the army's expertise—in a fortnight, and the university is assembling a team of volunteers to go over there in the next school holiday period—'

'Which is also in a fortnight,' Leonie put in. As a single mother of two teenagers, school holidays loomed large in her mind.

Susan nodded.

'Our boys are among the senior school students who have volunteered to go, and I wondered if I could be spared for a week during that period. I could set the hospital up again, check what equipment survived, order new stuff—'

'And keep an eye on Lachlan and Stewart at the same time,' Peter finished for her.

'Heavens! That's the last thing on my mind,' Susan told him. 'I'm delighted the university people will have that responsibility for a fortnight. The timing's coincidental because not having them at home for the holidays has left me free to do something useful over there.'

Katie listened to the ensuing discussion of rosters and timetables with only the barest minimum of attention. For some reason—being in this room again with Peter, probably—her mind had dredged up the feel of his hand on her leg, and her physical responses to a mere thought were distractingly acute.

She hadn't seen him since she'd plonked a tray with coffee, milk, sugar and a packet of sandwiches on this same table that evening and left with a string of feeble and barely coherent excuses.

'Katie? What about you? Would you do it?'

All heads turned towards her as Jack asked the questions.

Do what? she wondered, scrabbling around in her brain for some clue to the conversation.

'I know it's a last-minute arrangement, but the Rotary Club handle the bookkeeping and social arrangements so you won't have that extra burden.' Leonie offered the words placatingly, but they didn't help in any way. Rotary Club? Social arrangements?

'I think she tucks herself away over there to catch up on her sleep,' Peter teased, turning to smile at her before explaining, 'We're talking about finding a replacement candidate for this year's Queen of the Outback. Tracey Cox has just discovered she's pregnant and feels too sick to be partying on for another month.'

Queen of the Outback! Tracey pregnant? She'd been at school with Tracey.

Her mind spun feverishly.

'But Allysha could do it! Or Christa! Or Sally! Or Jane! You could do it yourself, Leonie; it's not as if it's only for single women, or a beauty contest or anything— Oh! I didn't mean. . .'

She stopped and shook her head, wishing that the thick folds of hair could cover her completely. Talk about putting her foot in it!

'You might remember when you talk about not needing beauty that I was the base contestant not that long ago.' Susan came to her rescue, smoothing her skirt over her heavy hips and smiling complacently. 'And some people think I'm very beautiful, don't they, Eddie?'

Everyone laughed at her threatening tone, and Jack took up the explanation.

'Christa did it last year, while Jane and Allysha are both pleading wedding plans. Besides, they do the Wyrangi and the island clinic runs. They're out of town four nights a fortnight,' Jack pointed out.

'But what about Sally, or one of the other girls from the visitors' centre?'

'My mum says I'm too young,' Sally said.

'And you can stop offering substitutes, Katie!' Peter put in firmly. 'You know the Service uses the contest not only to raise the extra money it needs to keep operating but also to showcase what we do here in Rainbow Bay.'

Katie tried to protest, but he held up his hand and continued, 'You've worked here for years—know more about what we do than most of the doctors—and, although it isn't a beauty contest, it doesn't hurt to have a good-looking woman representing us. In fact, I shall appoint myself as Queen consultant and escort when required.

'Give the Rotary Club her name, Leonie, tell them to send over the list of activities they've got planned for the final count-down to the big night and let's get back to the Coorawalla problem for a few minutes. Didn't you find out something about vaccines, Jack?'

She watched the heads all turn back towards the head of the table and didn't know whether to feel relieved or disappointed. Peter had supported the suggestion and offered to help so that they could get the minor business of the meeting out of the way as quickly as possible.

She would talk to Leonie later about the Queen idea. Surely she would be able to find someone else.

'There is a vaccine now against Japanese B encephalitis,' Jack explained, as Peter wondered what on earth had prompted him to get involved in the Queen of the Outback business. It might have reached the final count-down, but this last month could provide a round of social engagements that the Queen of England would find daunting!

Could he have been influenced by an unexpected pinkness in Katie's cheeks when she'd realised what they were discussing? Had there been a hint of pleasure amid her embarrassment and discomfort? He glanced at her again, hoping to confirm the impression, and was surprised by the clean symmetry of her profile as she pushed her heavy hair back behind one ear. He frowned, puzzled that he should be seeing things he'd never seen before. Had he always been unobservant? Had the brush with mortality during the cyclone sharpened his awareness of the world? Or only of Katie?

'Is Japanese B transmitted by mosquitoes?' Nick asked and Peter, realising that an important conversation was eddying around him, put aside all extraneous thoughts and concentrated on viral encephalitis.

'It is,' Jack replied, 'but the host animal is a monkey.

In the USA there is a California encephalitis, two forms of equine encephalitis—both carried by rats—and the one which most closely resembles ours—St Louis encephalitis. There, they have discovered, domestic fowls are the source.'

'And the authorities suspect waterfowl are our carriers,' Peter added, hoping that an intelligent contribution to the discussion might banish other uncertainties. 'I can see the relationship, although most of the people at Coorawalla also keep domestic birds— chickens, ducks, even guinea-fowl—for food and eggs. What's the answer? Kill all the pets?'

'Not really effective if the native birds still carry it,' Jack reminded him. 'Do you think recognising the symptoms early would prove useful? Or trying something like gamma globulin? Perhaps the immunisation effects of it would lessen the reaction of people to the virus.'

'I like that idea,' Peter said. 'If Susan and I could both go over we could take blood from the local men still on the island on our first day, and send all the samples back to the mainland for testing. If the hospital here can test all the people who've been evacuated we'll know who's carrying antibodies, and is therefore immune, and which people are still at risk. A gamma globulin injection for those still at risk won't hurt them.'

'Not much!' Susan told him. 'I had one when I was pregnant with the twins. It was before all girls were given rubella vaccinations at school and a friend came down with German measles. It was worse than childbirth, that needle,' she remembered feelingly.

'It would still be better than doing nothing,' Jack agreed. 'I'll talk to the boffins at the university and see what they think.'

'I agree it's worth a try. The eventual answer is a

type-specific vaccine,' Nick put in. 'There's no point in trying the Japanese B vaccine on the off chance that it might work. For one thing it could lead to complacency among the people and for another, by introducing another set of antibodies, we run an added risk of the new virus becoming live and then we'd have another killer on our hands.'

Peter shifted on his chair.

'So, we do our best to control the mosquitoes and try to impress on the entire population that they must cover up and use repellent,' he said. 'I don't know which of the two tasks is the most formidable on a hot, wet tropical island.'

'Well, if you and Susan could both go over for a week you could run an information campaign,' Nick suggested. 'Explain that the injection is not a vaccination and they will still be at risk, and drum the dangers into their heads until they have to take notice.'

'I could do that on my own,' Susan offered, but Jack shook his head.

'I know you and the other nurses probably do more hands-on work with these people than the doctors, but they still take more notice of a man. I'll look at the rosters and see what I can arrange. Perhaps if you had good radio contact and a plane we could run part of the on-call service from there. It would be like old times when all consultations were by radio.'

He shifted slightly in his seat to speak to Katie.

'Would you be willing to spend a week at Coorawalla with Susan and Peter if it was necessary?' he asked and Peter, curious to see what she would say, turned towards her and saw that faint colour creep into her cheeks again.

He studied her while she answered Jack's questions about the extra equipment they might need. She had to be twenty-three or -four, yet there was a freshness about her, an unworldliness, that was as rare as it was attractive.

Most of the women he knew were born worldly, he was sure! In fact, he'd started to think that it might be a new genetic development—they were so confident and assured and ready to take their rightful place in the world.

The phone rang, and Katie turned to answer it. She moved economically, Peter decided, swinging around in her chair with an easy grace. A curious disappointment flickered within him and he realised that he'd have liked the opportunity to study her for a little longer.

As if the noise of the phone had been a signal of some kind people stood up, moving away from the table. Peter waited until the others had gone, knowing that he was still impeded by his bound ankle and the crutches.

Jack had moved to sit beside Katie at the radio desk, both their heads bent as Jack listened and Katie wrote.

He'd have liked to talk to her about the Queen business, he thought, swinging himself out of the room with a vague feeling of dissatisfaction snapping at his heels.

Katie knew that he had gone. Even with her head bent over the list of medical supplies Jack was dictating, she had been aware of Peter's presence as surely as if he'd been touching her.

This is stupid, she told herself, crossing out 'detractor' and writing 'retractor' in its place. She'd had this nameless 'thing' she'd always hoped couldn't possibly be love about Peter since he began work at the base years ago but, apart from a strange lurch of her stomach when she saw him unexpectedly around the place, there'd been no physical symptoms of the 'condition'.

Yet, since Thursday, when she'd talked to him through the night, something had changed. Now she had only to hear his voice and her skin would tingle, and tissues inside her body—bits which had never had a life of their own before—would swell with a shivery kind of delight.

'Did you get down those small-bore needles and the suture thickness, Katie?' Jack asked, and she looked at him in shock, unable to believe that her thoughts had taken her so far away that she'd been oblivious to his voice.

What was going to happen? she wondered as she wrote down the final few items Jack dictated. A stomach lurch or two she could hide, but if she was going to be lured into ridiculous and unproductive daydreams by shivery swellings inside her body people would begin to wonder about her.

She was grateful when the phone rang again—and again. Work was the answer. And when she wasn't busy answering phones, she could go through the old radio manuals and see what equipment she would need at Coorawalla to ensure good reception and a stronger transmitting beam for the time she would be stationed there—if she was needed!

The treacherous reminder that Peter would also be there tried to slide into her mind, but she had her emotions back under control and she fought its intrusion with a concentrated effort.

'What will your parents think of this Queen of the Outback idea?'

It was late afternoon and she thought she'd said good-bye to all the staff as they hurried off to their other lives. She turned slowly from her desk, knowing that it was Peter in the room behind her and preparing her stomach not to lurch this time.

'I think they'll be surprised,' she answered honestly,

twisting in her chair to face him and instantly aware that her preparations were supremely unsuccessful.

'Only surprised?' he pressed, hobbling into the room and dropping into a chair by the big table. He was facing her now and close enough to touch if she reached out a hand.

'Well, Dad will probably be pleased as well,' she admitted. 'He doesn't say much but I think I've been a bit of a disappointment to him. He was very social when he was young. He wanted me to go south to university and see something of other places, but...'

'But you've always been a home-body,' he finished for her.

'I happen to like Rainbow Bay, I love my job and I have no yearning to go anywhere else,' she objected. 'But calling me a home-body makes me sound as stodgy as bread-and-butter pudding.'

She paused for a moment and was about to add, Perhaps I am, when Peter spoke again.

'Bread-and-butter pudding is back on the menus of all the top restaurants,' he said quietly, his voice triggering the shivery responses once again. 'Its basic ingredients and subtle blend of taste have turned it into a much-fancied choice among connoisseurs.'

She looked at him, trying to work out if he was making a culinary observation or saying something more. His blue eyes were grave and that, in itself, was different. Peter's eyes usually twinkled with mischief or shone with excitement. She'd seen them frown with concern over a problem, or spark with anger in a heated debate—but grave was something new. And definitely unsettling!

'Calling Rainbow Bay! This is VHK-38 on the trawler *Esmerelda*. Can you hear me, base?'

A woman's voice was on the radio, unrecognisable

but tight enough for Katie to feel a spark of fear along her nerves.

'I can hear you, *Esmerelda*, she said calmly. 'Go ahead.'

'Is a doctor there? My son has something caught in his throat. We've picked him up and thumped him and hugged him with our fists against his chest but it hasn't moved and his lips are turning blue. Should we do that operation?'

Katie rolled her chair to one side to make room for Peter at the desk. She heard him speak to the woman, introducing himself and asking Benny's age—his even, unemotional tone urging its own control.

She heard the replies but was wondering about 'that operation'. Once a year the School of Distance Education pupils came to the Bay for a camp, accompanied by their home tutor—usually a parent. Katie gave radio sessions for the home tutors and the doctors at the base held similar clinics, instructing the adults in first aid and talking about the equipment in the medical chest, which each isolated family received from the Government. Had they given instructions for emergencies like this?

'Benny's on the table, and my husband is holding him,' the woman said. 'We've got item 207—the swabs—ready, and the scalpel.' Her voice faltered as if the idea of thrusting such an instrument into her child's throat was more than she could handle. 'We've got the piece of tubing that we were told to keep and Elastoplast.'

'Will I alert the on-call staff?' Katie whispered, and saw Peter nod. He held up one finger, and she dialled the pager number which would send the pilot straight to the airport and tapped in the priority one alert signal.

She couldn't remember which doctor was on call,

but she knew that he would have the mobile phone with him.

'Feel for his Adam's apple,' Peter said calmly, while she waited for the phone to be answered. 'Remember how we did it in practice? How distinct it was? Remember the ridge you felt below it; can you feel that?'

Katie had been on the trawlers often enough to be able to visualise the cabin and, in her mind, the woman's face was white, her lips compressed as she fought to keep her hands steady. Then Nick's voice answered the phone, and she explained what was happening.

'Peter will phone you later,' she said, her stomach twisting into a knot with empathetic tension as he carefully guided the woman's hands with his words.

'Now, the first slit is up and down, between the Adam's apple and the next ridge, then the next slit is across. You'll feel air come out. Turn your scalpel upside down and use it to spread the edge of the wound apart and slide the tube in. You practised that on the dolls, remember.'

Katie felt her own lips compress, and her breathing stopped completely. She dialled the nurse's mobile and repeated the emergency evacuation message.

All the evac staff needed to know at this stage was to get to the airport as quickly as possible. A second phone call, while the plane was being rolled out and the pre-flight checks took place, would explain the emergency so that they would know what equipment they should take.

'She's got it in! His chest's moving.'

The man's voice was choked with tears, and Peter's sigh echoed her own release of air.

'Someone must hold it all the time,' Peter warned them. 'Where's your nearest port and how soon can you get there?'

'We can be in Wyrangi in less than an hour,' the man replied.

'Good going. I'll get the hospital sister to meet you at the wharf with oxygen. She'll arrange to take him straight to the airport and our plane should be there within half an hour of your arrival.'

The man repeated the instructions and again the cabin where the people stood was vivid in Katie's mind, their relief spinning through the air to bring a tiny smile to her lips.

'I'll stand by here in case you need to contact me again,' Peter added. 'Before you get under way, try to fix pillows or padding to support your wife's arm. Holding that tube is going to be extremely uncomfortable as her fingers will cramp and her muscles will ache. She must also keep an eye on Benny's chest movements. If she doesn't see it rising she can blow gently through the tube in the same way as she would perform mouth-to-mouth resuscitation.'

Peter sounded calm, unflappable! Had he helped amateurs through this operation so often that his pulse no longer pounded, his throat no longer dried, and his fingers no longer shook with anxiety?

She clasped her own shaking fingers in her lap, and licked her own dry lips.

'I'll get some coffee,' she murmured, standing up cautiously—unwilling to trust legs which had been tense with fear for the woman at the other end of the radio signal.

'In a minute,' Peter said. He reached out and grasped her arm. She knew it was only to stop her moving away, but his skin was warm against her coldness, and her body jerked as violently as if an electric current had passed swiftly through it.

'Who's on duty, do you know?' he asked.

She shook her head, unable to think of anything other than the feel of his fingers on her skin, and the galloping rhythm of her heart.

'Nick,' she said jerkily, after what seemed a too-long silence. 'And, I think, Christa.' She'd been thinking more about the child and his parents than who had answered the nurse's phone. 'I told Nick you'd call him on the mobile when you had a moment and fill him in on the medical details.'

'I'll ring him now,' he said quietly, but he didn't release her arm.

Pulling away from his hand, she hurried into the kitchen and put on the kettle to make coffee. It was the strain of listening to Peter's words which had caused her to react so violently to his touch, she told herself. She and Peter were colleagues and nothing had changed—in spite of the shared experience of one long, wild night.

'Jack and I have been trying to talk the Health Department into supplying emergency cricothyrotomy kits to families in isolated areas.'

Peter's voice brought her spinning around from the bench.

'Crico-whatsis?' She frowned as she tried to make sense of the word—to pretend that her thoughts were still as focussed on the patient as his obviously were. 'I thought the operation you talked the woman through was a tracheostomy.'

Peter nodded. He rested his crutches against the bench and ran the fingers of one hand through his hair, then smoothed it flat again with his palm.

'It's a similar thing,' he explained, moving awkwardly along the bench and reaching up for coffee and mugs. 'With a tracheostomy the cut is lower, directly into the trachea. Children have a much shorter trachea and there's a high mortality rate with tracheostomies performed on them. With a cricothyrotomy the incision is made into the larynx and there's slightly more leeway for error.'

Now he was pouring hot water into the coffee-pot and she watched the deft movements of his hands, forgetting that it was she who had offered to make the coffee—she who was more mobile at the moment and certainly should be doing it!

'What equipment is available in the emergency kits you and Jack want supplied?' she asked, and he glanced up and smiled at her.

'You like knowing all the details, don't you?'

Don't blush, she told her skin, but it didn't obey, reacting to the hint of admiration in his voice instead.

'The more I know, the easier it is for me to understand the kind of help people need,' she said carefully, trying to explain a difficulty which was hard to verbalise—and to keep her mind off the soft hairs on Peter's arms, lit to gold by the bright kitchen light. 'Some of the radio or phone calls I get bring their own special confusion. Things like, ''Johnny bit the dog and now he's foaming at the mouth; what can we do?''.'

Peter grinned.

'You made that one up,' he accused, and she shook her head.

'I did not. That mightn't have been the exact phrasing, but that was how it sounded to me.'

'And was the woman worried about the dog or Johnny?'

Peter pushed a mug of coffee along the bench towards her, then followed it with the milk and sugar. She concentrated on adding milk, so aware of his closeness that they could have been touching.

'The dog, of course,' she told him. 'She had six other

kids. But they were drovers and the dogs were like a carpenter's tools—essential to their livelihood.'

'And what expert knowledge did you bring to bear to sort it out?'

She glanced up at him and met his eyes, alight with interest and gleaming with suppressed laughter.

She smiled her response.

'That's the wrong question, you know,' she said. 'You should have asked if the dog recovered.'

He chuckled, and she added, 'Actually, I asked her where they were—the dog and Johnny. You know the RFDS *User's Guide* says to bring the patients as close to the radio or phone as possible? Well, sometimes they do that.'

' "They're right here," she said. "Mickey's got the dog, and Jamie's holding Johnny." '

' "Ask Johnny what he was doing when it happened," I said, and I could hear her talking to the children. Then I heard a loud walloping noise and a child screaming, dogs barking and other noisy indications of all hell breaking loose. Eventually she came back to the radio and told me she was sorry she'd wasted my time, then ended the transmission.'

'So you don't know what happened?' Peter said, obviously put out that her story had finished so abruptly.

She smiled again.

'I found out about six months later,' she relented. 'It seems Johnny had been trying to shave the dog with his father's razor and shaving-cream. The dog, quite understandably, objected and nipped at him and Johnny, not to be outdone, retaliated by biting back.'

'I don't believe a word of it,' Peter announced when he'd stopped laughing. 'You made it all up.'

'I did not!' Katie said, a strange lightness floating through her spirit as she stood in the familiar kitchen and laughed, most unfamiliarly, with Peter. 'But it wasn't a good explanation of why I like to know about medical details, was it?'

'Not particularly good,' he agreed, still smiling at her, 'but, if you bring your coffee back in near the radio, I'll tell you about the cricothyrotomy pack anyway! It's right you should be interested. After all, you hear us talking about these things all day every day.'

'I'll carry your coffee, too,' she offered, uncertain how to react to this kindly, more human version of Peter.

Or perhaps she was imagining the warmth in his voice, she told herself as she followed him back to the radio room.

'I phoned Joan at Wyrangi, then radioed the *Esmerelda* before I came into the kitchen,' he assured her when she sat down to flip through the book of call signs which was kept beside the radio. 'They know the plane's on the way.'

'I hope that reassures them,' Katie said, although she suspected that the family wouldn't relax until their child was in expert hands. Peter had seated himself beside her at the radio desk. Most of the staff sat there from time to time, using the phones or the radio. But most of them didn't make her feel uncomfortable in a prickly, jittery, unsettled kind of way.

Peter opened a book he must have picked up on his way back to the desk and pushed it towards her, moving closer so that his sleeve brushed against her arm.

'See this illustration of a child's throat,' he said, one long finger skimming over the page. 'Because of the risks involved in operations like this, a cricothyrotomy is only performed if there's a foreign body lodged in the larynx or in accident cases where there's severe damage to the face or to the larynx itself.'

Katie nodded, embarrassed that her hair was sliding forward and catching on Peter's shoulder.

'The woman made her incision here,' Peter explained. 'In the classes we use child-size dolls. We make them feel for the right place again and again until their fingers could do it in the dark. Now, she had to use a scalpel and actually cut through skin and membranes, but medical staff have an easier option these days. We would have performed a needle cricothyrotomy, using a special large-gauge angio-catheter—'

He glanced across at her face, as if checking to see whether she was following the explanation.

'Flexible, hollow tubes that slip down over a needle, Katie said, to let him know she understood. 'They are left in place in a vein or artery when the needle is taken out. I thought they were only used as fluid lines, either to infuse fluid or withdraw fluid. Of course, I can see that they could be used for air as well.'

Peter nodded.

'You can understand that using a needle and catheter to create an airway is a much simpler procedure than making an incision. With the needle, the operator has to clean the skin, locate the ridge of the membrane, put the needle on the midline and advance it at a forty-five degree angle towards the feet.'

Katie listened to the explanation as carefully as she could but her mind was distracted by Peter's fingers, moving all the time in a mime of the actions he was describing. She jerked her attention back from unprofitable speculation about those fingers. . .

'A syringe is attached to the hub of the catheter and, by keeping suction on the syringe, it is easy to tell when air is aspirated and the person performing the operation can stop exerting pressure. All that's left to do is to advance the catheter, remove the needle and there you have a dinky little tube in place.'

He turned his hands palms upwards, like a magician presenting himself for applause at the end of his act. She considered clapping, but felt it might trivialise his concise report.

'I'm sure you made it sound a lot easier than it is, but I can understand its appeal to a lay person caught in a situation where they had to do something drastic to save a life.'

Her heart sank when she heard the words come out. She sounded so prissy, so stuffy! Maybe it would have been better if she'd clapped after all.

The phone interrupted her pointless speculation.

'It's Joan, Katie. Tell Peter the *Esmerelda* is coming up against the wharf now. I can contact him by phone if there are any problems.'

Of course you can, Katie thought, depressed to think that this strange little interlude was about to end. She passed on the message, and handed Peter the mobile phone still on the radio desk.

'I'll close down here and let the after-hours service know we're going. If Joan rings, the call will automatically go through to that mobile.'

She didn't—couldn't—look at him in case he read the disappointment in her face.

'Well, hurry up,' he said briskly, pushing back his chair and standing up to swing above her on the crutches.

'Why?' she muttered, wanting him gone so that she could wallow—for a moment—in her misery.

'Because I'll be waiting for you,' he said with exaggerated patience. 'We've got to talk about this Queen thing—get you organised. I thought I'd drive you home, then we could discuss it with your parents as well. Do they eat pizza or Chinese food? Should we pick something up? I wouldn't want to put them out.'

She was glad that she was sitting down—it saved her from falling! And glad that he couldn't see her face, with her jaw hanging slackly open in an idiotic fashion.

'But you don't need. . .you don't have to. . . The Rotary Club. . .'

'Come on, Katie!' he urged, ignoring the morass of half-sentences which tangled off her tongue. 'Put your precious radio to bed and let's get out of here.'

She could tell that he was moving away from her because his voice was getting softer.

'Now, Chinese or pizza? If I phone an order through we won't have to wait for it.'

She heard someone say, 'Chinese,' but it couldn't have been her. She was sure that she'd been rendered speechless for life!

CHAPTER FOUR

KATIE's fingers fumbled with unaccustomed clumsiness as she switched their communication system through to the after-hours answering service. He's doing this so that you don't make a complete hash of the Queen business, she reminded herself. It's nothing personal and if you start thinking it is you're likely to make a fool of yourself.

With these last-minute instructions in the forefront of her mind she left the radio room, but the sight of Peter leaning nonchalantly against the wall in the corridor, clearly flirting with a woman on the other end of the phone, reminded her that her body was less easily persuaded, convinced or subdued.

'You're ready? Great! Let's go.'

He pushed himself away from the wall, unbalanced for a moment. Should she reach out and steady him? No! It was hard enough to control stomach lurches and heart flutters when he was in the same room, without touching him to make a complete farce of her efforts.

'I'll drive my car, and you can follow,' she said firmly, reasonably certain that sitting in the front seat of his little sports car with him would be nearly as bad as touching.

'But your car's not here,' he said, looking around the all but deserted car park.

Of course it wasn't. This morning had been fine and sunny—the first clear day since the cyclone called Jill had hit the Bay—and she had walked to work, revelling in the musty smell of the sun on the sodden ground and seeing anew the hundred shades of green in the lush tropical gardens bordering the road.

'Come on,' he said. 'Riding in an open sports car with the base Casanova won't plunge you straight into "fallen woman" status.'

She spun around to face him. Was that bitterness she heard in his voice? His lips were spread in a smile but the gleam wasn't there, in his eyes or on his skin, the way it usually was when he smiled.

'No one thinks of you that way,' she objected. 'The staff have far too much respect for you as a doctor to ever classify you that glibly.'

'And you, Katie?' he said, still serious. 'Are you part of this generalisation of "the staff"?'

She nodded, confused by a hint of emotion she could not identify in the deep timbre of his voice.

'You talk a lot of nonsense and tease and joke and flirt, but everyone knows you've as much dedication to doctoring and to the Service as Jack has. No one takes you lightly, Peter.'

She felt as if she were floundering around in the dark; as if Peter had become a stranger—a stranger in pain of some kind; a stranger who needed her help.

Then he smiled and the light returned as clear as sunshine after a cloud has crossed the sun.

'More generalisations, Katie!' he chided, waggling an admonitory finger in front of her nose. 'But I suppose that's all I can expect.'

He waved her towards the car with an awkward half-bow.

'Your carriage awaits, madam,' he added, with all the casual exuberance of the old Peter.

So why did she feel as if the earth had shifted under her feet? For a moment there an opportunity had opened up, then had closed too quickly for her to take advantage of something special she'd been offered.

She shook her head, telling herself that the nebulous thought made no sense whatsoever, and the sooner she returned from fantasy land and became 'feet on the ground' Katie again the better. Especially as she was about to sit in that very small sports car with him!

'But you're Bill Watson, the Australian five-eight!' Peter greeted her father a little later, with something approaching awe. She watched Peter balance himself while the two men shook hands.

How could she possibly get her feet back on the ground when Peter kept surprising her like this? As far as she knew no one in Rainbow Bay had the slightest interest in Rugby Union, and certainly not enough knowledge of its history to recognise her father as a legend of the past. She looked around the familiar room, wondering if she'd forgotten that there were photos of him in football gear somewhere around.

There weren't, of course!

'You shouldn't have let him bring all this food.' Her mother's plaint made her turn towards the dining-room table, where assorted dishes of Chinese delicacies had been transferred from plastic containers to classic Doulton serving bowls. A full dinner service of the beautiful china had been her mother's wedding present from her family. It was still used daily by the three of them, but now it seemed overdone to Katie.

Would it appear as if her mother was making too much of a fuss? she wondered, as the strangeness of having Peter in her home made her question everything.

'Would you believe Peter's father was such a fan of mine he still has an autographed programme of the 1954 test against Great Britain?'

I'd believe in Santa Claus at the moment, Katie thought, smiling weakly at her father's transparent delight. As he walked through to the kitchen to help her mother, she muttered to Peter, 'How could you possibly guess he was the footballing Bill Watson? There must be thousands of people in the world with that name.'

Peter looked surprised.

'I recognised him,' he murmured. 'He's older, of course, but he still has those strong facial features that made him such a pin-up boy when he was a young star. My mother always said he was the handsomest man she ever saw.'

He paused for a moment, looking intently at her with an unfathomable expression in his eyes.

'In fact, you look like him, you know.'

She felt another wash of colour start and turned abruptly away.

'Handsome enough to be a pin-up boy?' she muttered. 'Thanks a heap!'

'Can you manage to get over here with your crutches?' her mother asked, indicating a chair for Peter.

He smiled, and propped the crutches against the wall.

'I think they're becoming an affectation,' he said. 'I can actually hobble along quite well without them.'

Katie watched as he limped to his place, wincing as he put his injured foot to the floor. He looked up at her and winked and she looked hurriedly away, feeling an unexpected intimacy creeping over her.

Her father, she noticed, had produced a bottle of wine from somewhere and was peering suspiciously at it.

'I don't know if red or white is appropriate with Chinese food,' he said. 'This is a red I was given recently. The chap who gave it to me has a fine palate so it should be drinkable.'

He passed it to Peter, who glanced at the label and then whistled appreciatively.

'It should be more than just drinkable, sir,' he said, passing the bottle back. 'I've never been privileged to taste it, but I've heard it spoken of with great reverence.'

Her father chuckled, obviously delighted by Peter's complimentary reply.

I can understand how Alice felt in Wonderland, Katie thought. This is as unreal as any tea-party with the Mad Hatter and his friends. She sat in her usual place at the table, trying to ignore the fact that Peter was directly opposite her. Peter the Playboy who, for three long years, had been a very secret ache in her heart.

'You were caught in the cyclone that hit the island in the gulf, weren't you, Peter?' her mother asked, holding a bowl of fried rice towards their guest. 'Is that how you hurt your ankle?'

'Yes to both questions. The ankle was a minor mishap, but being trapped was a frightening experience. I know I have Katie to thank for my sanity,' he replied, smiling across the table so warmly that Katie wanted to kick him. She didn't want her parents to start thinking. . .!

Her mind boggled at what they might start thinking. They might be unworldly in some ways, but—

'She talked to me through a long and lonely night.'

As she shuffled uncomfortably on her seat she saw her father's quick glance. His unspoken, 'Katie talk all night?' hovered in the air above the table.

'I was only doing my job,' she said flatly, hoping to defuse the celebratory atmosphere which had permeated the room. 'In fact,' she added, 'it's because of the job that Peter's here. They. . .er. . .' Suddenly this explanation was harder than she thought it would be. Because Peter was there, she was sure! 'Everyone else is getting married or pregnant or done it before,' she said nervously, 'so they want me to fill in for the girl who was the base entrant in the Queen of the Outback quest.'

By this time her heart was thumping so hard that she thought they must all hear it, and her cheeks so hot that she knew they would be scarlet with embarrassment.

'They want you because you'll be the best person for the job, Katie,' Peter corrected firmly.

Her mother murmured, 'That's nice, dear,' and her father's eyes twinkled with delight.

'You don't object, Mr Watson? Mrs Watson?'

'Why should we object?' her father said. 'Katie's a grown woman; she makes her own decisions. I would have thought all the people who worked with her would have realised that by now.'

Which was as close as my father will come to saying I'm stubborn, Katie thought bitterly, forking food into her mouth with great concentration and hoping they would think her oblivious to the conversation.

'You're thinking, I suppose, that as a minister I might have moral objections,' her father said, and she forgot the pretence of eating and looked up at him and smiled.

She loved both her parents dearly, but her father's habit of cutting straight to the truth of matters never failed to delight her. True, it had made her uncomfortable at times when she was younger, but these days she admired his frankness and tried to emulate it when she could.

She turned to Peter, who had been sipping at his wine when her father spoke, and watched as he returned the glass to the table.

'I did think you might have reservations,' he admitted.

'And that's why you brought Katie home? You were going to provide back-up services in persuading us that she would not be plunged into moral turpitude?'

Katie could see her father's lips twitching and knew

that he was teasing Peter. She looked at their guest, feeling like an onlooker at a tennis match—her attention switching from one player to the other.

'I brought her home because we were both working late, and I hadn't had a chance to talk to her about this Queen thing. Although the Rotary Club members say they will do all the work, I know from past experience that the contestant has to rush about all over the place and her family are often inconvenienced.'

He had turned towards her mother as he spoke, and he smiled at her. 'I've been involved before,' he explained. 'The girls often need an escort—particularly at the out-of-town race days or rodeos. Both as a precautionary medical measure and because most of the money raised is donated to the RFDS, we send a plane and medical staff to the bigger functions. I'm the volunteer for the job this year.'

'And you'll guide her through final month,' her mother said placidly. 'It's very kind of you, Peter. You'll have to see what clothes you've got, Katie,' she added, 'if there's to be a rash of socialising.'

Katie's stomach sank and her attention switched to her maternal relative. Her mother rarely made remarks about anyone's personal appearance, but including clothes and Peter in the same conversation implied something which made her blush internally.

Peter must have made some reply but she'd missed it, and now her father was adding his advice.

'And cut down on your other activities,' her father said. 'As Peter said, it's only for a month but if you agree to do the job you'll have to commit yourself to it one hundred per cent. I imagine it will be a fairly demanding schedule?'

He turned enquiringly towards Peter, looking for back-up.

'I know that, Dad,' she interjected quickly, embarrassed at being the centre of attention. It was hard enough handling the eccentricity of having Peter in the house without fielding her parents' random remarks about her clothes or pastimes as well. Certain that she had to divert them, she looked across the table at Peter and asked, 'Did your father play rugby, that he was such a fan?'

Had he seen the appeal in her eyes? Would he catch the conversational ball she'd flung in desperation?

'He played at university, but didn't go further than that,' Peter replied. 'He's also a doctor, and found he was so busy during the first years as a resident, then registrar and on through the slow climb towards specialising that he had little time for anything else.'

Katie was diverted from her own discomfort by a sharp edge in Peter's usually casual tones. Had his father been too busy for his children? she wondered, but it was too personal a question to ask.

'It has always been difficult for young men trying to establish themselves to make time for everything,' her father remarked, honing in on the essence of the conversation.

'Today we hear a lot of talk about time management and people excuse themselves for spending less time with their children by calling the time they do spend "quality time", but the problem of juggling careers and families doesn't change. It's a great pity because a father's influence in his children's lives is as important as a mother's, if only men could realise it.'

'My father's influence was strong enough,' Peter said almost abruptly, then his voice softened slightly as he added, 'He always took me to the interstate rugby matches and the tests, although I was too young to have seen you play.'

The talk turned back to football and then to Peter's career but Katie, alert to every cadence in Peter's voice, knew that some of the exuberance with which he'd greeted her father had dissipated. Was he uncomfortable in this family atmosphere or had all the personal talk made him feel that he was being viewed as a suitor?

Surely not! her mind shrieked.

It was another hour before they left the table—an hour of agony for Katie as she tested every innocently asked question for ulterior motives. Peter's offer to help with the dishes was greeted with laughter and jokes about broken crockery, and when he said he had better be going her parents said goodbye. Her mother added, 'Katie will see you out.'

Her father shook hands with Peter and said, 'Do come again any time,' with his usual politeness.

They then disappeared tactfully into the kitchen.

'I'm sorry, Peter,' Katie muttered as she walked slowly through the garden with him. 'I hope they didn't give the impression that they thought you were courting me. It's just that I've never brought anyone—' not entirely true, she realised, but couldn't bring herself to say 'any man' '—from work home with me before. I love them both dearly, but at times their curiosity about other people's lives. . .'

'Don't apologise for them, Katie. I found them both delightful and entertaining company.'

Again her auditory sense honed in on a brusqueness in his voice but before she could question it he had stopped and turned towards her, his wide shoulders blotting out the light from a waning, misshapen moon.

'It's natural they should be interested in your fellow workers,' he said quietly, 'but we didn't get much Queen discussion done, did we? Perhaps we could talk about that over the dinner I promised you.'

Go out to dinner with Peter? Her head spun! It would give her parents more wrong ideas, not to mention the possible consequences to her heart and the shivery bits of her body. She snatched a quick breath and blew it out in a sigh, knowing that she couldn't stand in a speechless trance much longer.

'Unless you're too busy with your ''other activities'',' he murmured, swaying a little closer to her and escalating her awareness of his physical appeal.

'No. . . Yes. . . Oh, I don't know!' she said. 'We have to talk about it all, I suppose, but couldn't we discuss it at work?'

What she really wanted to do was to move away from him, but her body had ceased obeying even the simplest of instructions.

'I promised you dinner,' he said patiently. 'I'm free Wednesday, Thursday and Friday nights.'

Not Saturday! she thought, stupidly disappointed. Saturday was 'going out' night—with girlfriend or boyfriend, not with an acquaintance from work!

'Wednesday, then,' she answered ungraciously. 'We might as well get it over and done with.'

Even with his face shadowed, she sensed his reaction and heard a smile in his voice when he replied, 'Your parents certainly wouldn't think it was a courtship if they'd heard that reluctant reply, Katie.'

The words shamed her, and she looked into his deep-shadowed eyes.

'I'm sorry,' she said, shaking her head. 'You're putting yourself out, offering to help, to be an escort and tell me what to expect. I'm behaving very badly about it all.'

He didn't move, and she could almost feel his eyes studying her in the silvery moonlight. Uncomfortably aware of what such scrutiny might reveal, she moved away—walking on towards the gate and then pausing in the shadow of a large jacaranda to wait for him.

'Blasted crutches!' he muttered as he drew level. With agile skill he moved closer to the tree and leant back against the trunk, rubbing at his shoulders as if they were aching from the unaccustomed weight of his body. 'I'll use a walking-stick if I have to, but these things go tomorrow. Have you any idea how limiting they are?'

She was puzzled by his conversation but moved closer to him, wondering if she could help in some way. He reached out and pushed her hair back from one side of her face, tucking the weight of it behind her ear. His fingers brushed her temple and slid along her skin, and she clenched her teeth to stop the trembling it caused.

'Is there a special man in your life who's going to be upset about my involvement?' he asked abruptly. 'Is that what's worrying you?'

She shook her head again, too distracted by his touch to answer immediately. But she knew she had to answer in case he should suspect. . .

'It was all dumped on me so suddenly,' she said. 'And I'm not a Queen type of person—not a public kind of person, I mean.'

'So think of the challenge!' he said.

'I *am* thinking of it!' she groaned, thinking of two challenges, in fact—one was surviving a month of festivities, and the other was surviving a month of closer association with Peter than she needed.

'You'll be brilliant,' he predicted. 'And I'd better be going or your parents' suspicions about my role in your life will be rising again.'

He paused for a moment, and she realised that she didn't want him to leave. She was too practical a person to dream about impossibilities, but she couldn't deny her body's delight in his closeness.

'Of course, if I were a suitor,' he continued in the same level voice he'd used to say that he must leave, 'we wouldn't be talking, would we? We'd be closer together, and I'd be saying goodbye like this.'

She had barely absorbed his words when his hands drew her closer. His head bent and his lips touched her forehead, her nose, her closed eyelids and then—her heart thudding, breath held tightly—her lips.

Heat surged through her body, so intense that she felt it glowing in her skin. Did she stagger with the force of her reaction that Peter clasped her arms more tightly and held her steady?

Had he moved again that their bodies were now pressed together? And what had prompted her lips to open beneath his as if eager to absorb all she could of him? Was it to make the most of what might be a fleeting aberration on his part, but could be a lifetime jewel of memory for her?

The heat was dancing in her body now. If she could make her brain work she might even be able to name the tune that spun it to a frenzy. Her fingers clung to Peter's hair—although she couldn't remember giving the instructions that had twined her arms around his strongly muscled back.

Fingers in his hair? Arms around his back? Being kissed by Peter was one thing, but kissing him back was altogether different! She drew her hands back towards her body, balanced them against his chest, then told herself to ignore the warmth, the beating of his heart, the rise and fall of his lungs and push.

She pushed, then was grateful that he held her steady as they parted—and thankful that the tree-trunk was there to steady him. She'd forgotten his unsteadiness as she battled her own.

'But you're not a suitor,' she reminded him, pleased

to find her voice was working quite strongly. 'Goodnight.'

She waited until he had balanced himself on his crutches again, then turned and walked away—one hand pressed to her thundering heart and the other trying to cool her feverish cheeks. Determined not to run, she headed towards the sanctuary of her home.

'You'll have two days to get back to normal,' she told her reflection in the bathroom mirror, a reflection which looked most unfamiliar with delicately flushed skin softening the well-defined cheek-bones and emotion making her hazel eyes darker and somehow mysterious. 'Because,' she added to the stranger, 'he'll be on a clinic flight until Wednesday evening—'

Wednesday evening! She'd already said she would go to dinner with him. Could she get out of it somehow?

Not without lying! She'd agreed to Wednesday, not only because it would get the dinner over and done with but because it was the one free evening in her own busy schedule.

And her father was right—she'd have to think about how she could rearrange her other activities to make time for the Queen business. At least thinking about that should take her mind off Peter's kiss, she decided as she went to bed.

But she found it hard to concentrate on juggling her netball fixtures, coaching commitments and volunteer work at the native animal refuge when her body was still inflamed by Peter's kiss and her mind agitated by the strength of her response to it.

'Katie, do you know a vet you could call for some unofficial advice?'

One day was already gone and, judging by her body's reaction to Peter's voice on the phone, she hadn't succeeded in the 'getting back under control' department.

'I've a friend who would help,' she told him, although she didn't like asking favours of Richard. 'What do you need to know?'

'A small boy has brought his dog in,' Peter explained. 'He keeps looking at me with these huge brown eyes and expecting me to help him.'

'The boy or the dog?' she asked, half smiling as she remembered their earlier conversation.

Her heart began its fluttering again when she heard his deep chuckle.

'The boy this time,' he said. 'I have no idea what to do, but can't bear the thought of disappointing him.'

He was whispering now, as if the child and the dog were in the same room.

'She has a new litter of puppies, and I'd say it's probably mastitis,' he added in a louder voice. 'Her eyes look dull, her nose is dry and her teats seem hard and hot. I could try human antibiotics but I don't want to make her sicker. And I don't know what to do about the pups. Women keep nursing if they can cope with the pain, but dogs. . .'

'I'll give you Richard's number,' she said. 'It would be best if you phone him direct—that way he can ask you the questions he needs to ask without a third person relaying messages.'

She gave him the number, and waited while he repeated it.

'A number you know off by heart, Katie?' he murmured.

Her heart thudded harder.

'He's a friend,' she reiterated. 'I hope he can help.'

She said goodbye and hung up the phone, then lifted her hands above the desk and watched them shaking.

'This can't go on,' she said, then wondered about

connections between soliloquy and madness.

It was certainly madness, this sudden upsurge in her feelings towards Peter. Dreams were one thing, but when they started to intrude into reality they must be forgotten—banished—cast away for ever!

As Peter listened to the phone ringing, he wondered why he felt put out that Katie had known the number. Could it be connected to the fact that he'd phoned Katie for advice, rather than a vet he had used once before when a property manager had asked him to look at a sick bull? Could he have wanted to talk to Katie?

He shifted uncomfortably in his chair, willing someone to answer the phone before too many memories of that one surprising kiss surfaced from his subconscious. Surely that's how first kisses always felt, he told himself, trying to recall feeling that startling rush of heat—that mind-numbing explosion of desire—some time in the past. With someone!

'Richard Clewes's surgery,' a female voice announced, diverting him from his unsuccessful mental scanning of past romantic experiences.

He explained who he was and thought he detected a sniff when Katie's name was mentioned, but eventually he was put through to the vet.

'Definitely mastitis,' Katie's Richard told him. 'Any broad-spectrum antibiotic should help, but cut down the dosage according to the body weight of the animal in the same way as you would with a child. The problem will be keeping the puppies alive. When were they born?'

Peter turned to the small boy who sat on the ground, his pet's head resting on his knee.

'When did she have the puppies?' he asked.

The boy frowned up at him for a moment.

'Day before the day before yesterday,' he worked out. 'Eight she had, all exactly like her.'

Eight more like this poor, scrawny, indeterminate breed of dog? He decided that perhaps she had a nice nature, and passed on the necessary information.

'They'll need milk of some kind,' Richard told him. 'Do you people carry any baby formulas?'

'I'm sure I could find some,' Peter said.

'Good. Show the boy how to mix it at half-strength. Would you have baby bottles as well?'

How did I get myself into this? he wondered, listening to his own voice assenting yet again.

'Then work out the weight of the pups and mark the bottle with the amount the boy should give each of them each feed. He might have to draft in some of his mates to help. Let him have two or three bottles, if you can spare them. And tell him to keep the mother away from the pups. If they keep tugging at her nipples she could develop abscesses and that would be much harder to handle.'

'How long will this feeding regime go on?' he asked. 'He's a very small boy.'

'Look, if you don't think he can cope take the pups away from him now,' Richard said sharply. 'Either find homes for them wherever you are, explaining to the people who take them what will be involved in caring for them, or bring them back here with you. Katie usually cares for orphaned wild animals but she, or one of our other volunteers, would take them on.'

For some reason an image of Katie surrounded by eight starving and ugly puppies came into his mind, and Peter smiled as he thanked the vet and looked down at the small boy. He had another four hours at Herd Island, and he had a feeling that he was going to be the 'friend' drafted in to help. He repeated the information about keeping the mother away and bottle-feeding her brood.

'Do you want to keep the puppies?' he asked.

'Mum says I can't but I don't want them drownded,' the child replied, his eyes shining suspiciously again.

'I'll take one.'

He looked up to see Christa standing in the doorway. Her well-baby clinic must have finished early.

'And my friends will take two—one each,' the boy said, 'but you'll have to tell them about the feeding.'

'I could do that,' Christa said, coming over to kneel beside the boy and stroke the dog's head, then gently palpate her swollen teats. She looked up at Peter. 'Have you got anything you could give her for the mastitis?'

'If I'd known you diagnosed dogs I'd have saved myself a phone call,' he said, and reached into his drug case for antibiotics. 'Have you finished for the day?'

'Case notes to write up, then I've an antenatal clinic at two—only two women, as far as I know.'

Peter smiled and handed her the antibiotics.

'Could you work out a dosage of these based on the dog's body weight and write it out for the boy, then rustle up some baby formula and do the same with the puppies' weight? Give away any puppies you can, and I suppose we'll have to take the rest back to the Bay.'

Oblivious of the mess it was likely to make of her uniform, Christa lifted the dog.

'Katie will take care of them until they're big enough to be given away,' she said casually as she accompanied the boy out the door.

Did everyone know more about Katie than he did? he wondered, staring after Christa and the child.

Then he wondered why that bothered him.

CHAPTER FIVE

KATIE perused the list of activities supplied by the Rotary Club with a growing uneasiness. With only a month to go before the final event, it seemed that every affiliated organisation in their RFDS region was vying to put on some extra activity. She carried the list through to Leonie's office.

'I can't possibly go to all these functions,' she said, waving the piece of paper in the air before thrusting it towards the base manager. 'Most of the places are tiny dots on the map. How would I get there? When would I have time to work? Fund-raising is one thing, but this is ridiculous!'

Leonie smiled at her. It had an immediate calming effect, Leonie's smile, and Katie slipped into a chair across the desk and smiled back.

'Well, I couldn't get to most of them, could I?' she said, watching as Leonie read down the list.

'One important thing about the Queen of the Outback quest is that it publicises the Flying Doctor Service.' Leonie looked up from the list and leaned forward a little, as if to give extra emphasis to what she was saying.

'But, even more importantly, it gives the people in isolated places who rely on us for medical services an opportunity to say thank you in a practical way. By organising balls, or card days, or street stalls or picnic races they are doing their bit to keep the Service operating and, for people who do not like taking something for nothing, this is very important.'

'So my going to a card day in Castleford or a "cattle stampede" at Caltura helps keep their pride intact?' Katie smiled now, and Leonie nodded.

'But, being country people, they have a wealth of common sense. If you check the list against our clinic flights you'll find each town or property will hold their function either when the Service is there or on the weekend following a clinic so that the flight staff and the pilot can stay on for it.'

'Then, if flight staff are already in town representing the Service, I don't need to go,' Katie suggested, grasping at a possible opportunity to wriggle out of some of the frivolity listed on the daunting schedule.

'Of course you need to go,' Leonie told her firmly. 'You have to meet the other contestants and provide a bit of glamour.'

'Glamour? Me? The original blouse and skirt girl?' She looked ruefully down at her serviceable navy skirt and crisp navy and white striped shirt—clothes she was comfortable wearing.

'You look fine for work,' Leonie told her. 'Anonymous—self-effacing—exactly how you like to look!'

'Ouch!' Katie yelped as Leonie's unexpected probe hit home. She looked down at the skirt again. 'It's practical,' she defended weakly.

'I know,' Leonie assured her, 'and when you first started work here and were very young and very shy it helped you blend into the background.'

She looked up, catching Katie's grimace of embarrassment.

'But you're no longer a shy young girl, Katie,' she continued. 'You're an extremely capable and competent young woman and, beneath that hair, and behind your skirt and blouse image, a most attractive one. You must remember that the people we serve don't have a lot of glamour or excitement in their lives.

'That's why they love getting involved with the Queen of the Outback quest, love seeing ''their'' candidate in person and taking pride in her. And this year they've been disappointed. Poor Tracey has been sick for weeks and has missed many of the activities.'

'But they'll be more disappointed when they see me. I'll never be glamorous,' Katie objected, although she could understand the point Leonie was making.

'Leave it to Peter,' Leonie said kindly, rendering Katie speechless. 'Logan's Boutique in town donates our candidate's wardrobe, and they're happy to set you up with clothes for the remaining functions. Peter will know what will suit you and what won't.'

'You want me to go to Logan's Boutique with Peter, and try on clothes and parade in front of him and have *him* select what I should and shouldn't wear?' Katie exclaimed in horror.

Leonie looked puzzled, as if she couldn't find any objections to this scheme.

'But you must admit he's a woman's man, Katie. He knows these things. He's done it before, you know.'

'Well, he won't be telling me what to wear,' Katie muttered rebelliously. 'May I have the afternoon off?'

Leonie agreed so promptly that afterwards Katie wondered if she'd been set up.

Surely not, she told herself an hour later, watching in trepidation as the hairdresser removed thick handfuls of her ash-brown hair.

'I don't want it short short,' she told the woman, who smiled reassuringly at her reflection.

'I'm cutting it to chin length,' she said. 'With your facial shape a straight-cut bob will look great. You can push it back off your face with a band or clip it back, and when you want to look festive you take these side pieces up to the top of your head and use a fancy slide or ribbon to hold it in place.'

Katie stared at her reflection, her wide-apart eyes dominating the face so ruthlessly revealed.

'I like that look,' she heard herself say, then wondered if maybe she was sickening for something. Part of her was definitely uneasy about this transformation.

'So, the butterfly has finally emerged from its chrysalis,' Peter murmured when she opened the door to him that evening.

He was holding a box in his hands and had a plastic shopping bag slung over one arm, but she was far too nervous to ask about these unexpected burdens.

'I had my hair cut, that's all,' she told him. There was no need for him to know that she had spent two agonising hours in Logan's trying to decide what clothes a Queen contestant might need. And a further hour in an accessories store, selecting clips and pretty slides and colourful bands for her hair. 'I saw the schedule today and realised I'll have time to wash it about twice in the next month. I'm thinking of buying a selection of wigs.'

He laughed at her feeble attempt at humour, and she relaxed—slightly!

'Come in,' she offered, realising that he was still hovering on the doorstep.

'Perhaps I'd better explain the box first,' he suggested. 'You might prefer to shut the door politely in my face.'

He juggled the box while he put the plastic bag down, then he set the cardboard carton on the floor and opened it gingerly.

'They've just been fed,' he explained. 'Which is the only reason they're sleeping. Usually they are trying to get out, or crying so loudly you can't hear yourself think.'

Four tiny brown puppies were nestled in the folds of what she recognised as one of Peter's shirts. She knelt by the box and reached out a finger, touching one of them gently, then she looked up at Peter.

'The boy with the big brown eyes?' she asked softly.

He didn't reply immediately, but stood looking at her with a puzzled expression on his face—vague and frowning, like someone emerging from a long sleep.

'Yes,' he said slowly, then he shook his head as if to clear it and added more strongly, 'We managed to find homes for four of them.'

'I'll take them through to the kitchen,' she said, lifting the box from the floor and leading him into the house. 'Mum will keep an eye on them while I'm out. She's used to having stray animals dumped on her.'

Peter limped after her. He should have carried the box but he'd been so distracted there for a moment that she'd picked it up before he had time to object. It wasn't just the hair—he was certain of that. It was something deeper—as if the Katie he had known for years had suddenly split in two. The familiar Katie chatted to him about little boys with brown eyes, while the other one danced with a siren's enticement in his head.

'Hello, Peter.'

Mrs Watson's greeting brought him back to his senses and he managed to respond appropriately, but he glanced at Katie as she knelt to slide the box into a corner by the kitchen stove and tried to banish his wild fantasies with common sense.

She was wearing a cream linen sheath dress, and he knew enough about women's clothes to know that she had probably made it herself. It was totally unadorned, yet it suited her surprisingly shapely figure. A statuesque figure, he decided as she stood up and smoothed the dress down over her thighs. Full breasted, slim waisted, with gently swelling hips—he stopped abruptly. Thinking about Katie's hips was no way to banish fantasies!

'Shall we go?' she suggested, turning to him, her hazel eyes hiding her thoughts and feelings as effectively as a cat's solemn regard.

I should never have kissed her, he told himself as he said goodbye to Mrs Watson and walked out of the kitchen. Kisses had a tendency to upset the balance in working relationships. It had been an impulse of the moment—but he had never behaved impulsively with his female fellow workers before! And he'd be a liar if he said that he regretted the kiss! His body stirred—

'Did Richard suggest I look after the puppies?'

Katie's question broke into his capricious thoughts.

'Yes, he did,' he replied abruptly, and heard Katie sigh in response. Sighing for the unknown Richard? he wondered bleakly, and tried to imagine a face to fit around the voice he'd heard on the phone.

Would it give Richard an excuse to come visiting again? she wondered, battling the now-familiar guilt which thinking of Richard always invoked.

They reached the car, and Peter opened the door for her. Forgetting Richard, she slid cautiously into her seat—anxious to avoid accidental contact with any part of his body. That way, surely, she could control her reactions!

'I've booked a table at the Callistemon,' Peter told her, mentioning a popular restaurant set high on the cliffs at the southern end of the bay.

'So it wasn't blown away in the cyclone?' Katie joked, settling into the warm leather upholstery and deciding to try for a light and breezy approach to the outing.

'No,' Peter replied, 'much to the chagrin of the more pessimistic locals.'

As he spoke Katie sensed a relaxation in Peter, and felt the tension ease from her own contracted muscles. In spite of her silly physical reactions to Peter they could still meet and talk as friends. She began to list the activities planned for the month, and the subject of the quest got them safely to the restaurant and through the meal.

'Now, what about clothes?' Peter mentioned as they sat over coffee.

Katie stiffened, muscles knotting once again at the thought of parading clothes in front of Peter.

'I'm sure I can handle that,' she said, the words as hard and sharp as gravel chips.

Peter smiled at her.

'I put that badly, Katie,' he said. 'I know it seems rude to suggest to a woman that she might not know what clothes to buy but, having seen the different functions and knowing the places where they are held, I can sometimes offer advice about what's suitable and what's not.'

'Suitable?' she echoed frostily.

'Suitable!' he repeated. 'Not as in OK for a country town. You've enough taste and discretion to know that. I mean suitable for a ''cattle stampede'' at Caltura, where the locals will expect you to have your photo taken on a horse, and jeans and a checked shirt will please them a lot more than tailored trousers or trendy jodhpurs and a conservative cream blouse.'

The question of clothes slid right out of her mind.

'Photo taken on a horse?' she echoed weakly.

'About three times at least,' he told her.

'Do they hold the horse?' she muttered. 'At both ends?'

Peter threw back his head and laughed, the infectious sound banishing her trepidation as it sent a tingling delight down her spine. She looked at him, seeing the smooth, strong column of his throat revealed and the white ridges of taut tendons. Her stomach did its familiar lurching trick as her body escaped from the control she'd exerted on it all evening.

'I take it you don't ride?' he said, when he'd stopped laughing.

'Not on horses,' she told him emphatically.

'But, from what I've heard today, you're an animal lover!'

'I'm a small-animal lover,' she pointed out, pleased to have a conversation she could concentrate on once again. 'A horse is a very large animal, with one end that bites and another end that kicks.'

He chuckled again, but she had herself back under control and could watch the play of light on his smooth cheeks and quirking lips without more than a faint tremor of excitement in her veins.

'I'll undertake to hold all horses,' he promised solemnly, but laughter still lurked in the blueness of his eyes and Katie's soul sighed with a secret wish that he could laugh like this with her for ever.

'But do you understand what I mean about clothes?' he added, bringing the conversation back to the subject of the quest—to the reason they had met.

Katie nodded. She understood but had definitely not resigned herself to a shopping trip with Peter.

'I do,' she told him, 'so let's go through the list of activities and you can tell me what I'll need for each.'

He looked at her for a moment and she sensed that he was about to say something or ask her something.

The air grew tense, and it was an effort to breathe as his eyes conveyed messages which made her nipples tingle. Then he blinked, shook his head and reached forward to pick up her list.

'Have you got another piece of paper?' he asked, pulling a pen from his shirt pocket.

She found a notebook in her handbag and passed it to him, withdrawing her fingers too quickly when they touched his so that it fell onto the table between them.

He gave her another indecipherable look, then retrieved it.

Stupid! That was stupid! she scolded herself. The last thing you want is Peter suspecting he has an unnerving effect on you. Her mind picked up the 'unnerving', and repeated it mockingly in her head.

'Wyrangi is hot and humid, and you'll be taken out on one of the fishing boats,' Peter was saying when she dragged her thoughts back to the business of clothes. 'You'll need shorts and rubber-soled shoes, a hat and plenty of sunscreen. Nelly Gervase always puts on a big dinner at the hotel when the entrant's in town, which means wearing a dress—not too formal, but not so informal that the locals and the women from the prawning fleet feel overdressed.'

Not informal? Not overdressed? The scenario he was describing made her confusion at Logan's seem negligible.

'Maybe you'd better come with me,' she muttered, giving in reluctantly as she realised how little she knew of the social mores of the area the Service covered. She could understand now how important what she wore would be to the people she was representing, but it didn't make the idea of shopping for clothes with Peter any easier!

Peter talked about the places she would be visiting

as he drove her home, but the relaxed atmosphere had vanished. Signals from his body plucked at her nerves like careless fingers at violin strings, causing a discordant uneasiness inside her.

As he drew up outside her house she had the door open almost before the car stopped.

'Thank you very much for dinner and all the advice,' she gabbled as she scrambled out. 'I'll see you at work tomorrow.'

'A planned escape, Katie? There was no need for that,' he said quietly. 'I wasn't going to kiss you again.'

So there! she told herself, but when he said, 'Goodnight, Katie,' in a voice so low and soft that it brushed across her twanging nerve-endings she wished she'd waited in the car; talked a little longer—anything to prolong the pleasure-pain a few moments longer.

Peter drove away, wondering why he'd said such a stupid thing. It had probably hurt her feelings. Apart from anything else, she was the last person in the world he'd want to hurt.

On top of that was the fact that he wasn't certain that the remark had been honest. True, he'd decided earlier that there'd be no goodnight kiss. He kept his kisses for women who wanted a relationship and commitment as little as he did. Women who understood his dedication to his work, and knew that all he sought was pleasant company and relaxation—perhaps even a light-hearted affair which went nowhere and hurt no one.

But as for not kissing her again? He'd spent most of the evening longing to do just that, watching the way her lips moved as if he could work out the mechanics of the magic they'd so fleetingly provided.

Magic? Kisses? Katie? He must be entering a premature senility, or was he letting the recent tumultuous changes in his life affect his sanity? Not that she hadn't suddenly become infinitely kissable, but. . .

He braked at a roundabout and then accelerated out of it, but the familiar roar of power from the little sports car's engine failed to supply more than a momentary thrill. He felt restless—uneasy!

He considered calling in to see Jack, then wondered if that was becoming a habit—two bachelors sitting around late at night discussing work when two other men would probably have been discussing women.

He turned the car around but, instead of driving towards the Esplanade and The Bay Towers where Jack lived, he drove back towards Katie's house. Maybe, on such a fine, clear, star-filled evening, she had lingered in the garden. He could join her for a little while and apologise for his stupid remark. They could talk a while, and maybe things would slip back into their proper perspective.

She wasn't in the garden!

He knew that because he could see a light in what must be her bedroom; see her shadow moving behind closed blinds. Not clearly, of course, but he knew that it was her. He drove slowly past then accelerated again, telling himself that he'd enjoyed the evening because she was a friend—because he didn't have to make an effort to impress or entertain her. And that he didn't regret not kissing her!

Katie walked to work again, stretching out her stride and putting every ounce of energy she could muster into the exercise. Four demanding puppies had left her little time for sleep, and when she had seized a break between feeds she had slept badly—fantasy and dreams merging into nightmares where she twirled endlessly in front of Peter in a succession of ball-gowns, whirling faster and faster until she knew she would never be able to stop.

She had left the problem of the puppies with her parents, and today she would put all thoughts of the quest out of her mind, and concentrate on work, she promised herself, settling at her desk and phoning to advise the answering service that she was now on duty.

'Katie? This is Helen Jensen at Castleford.'

The call followed so swiftly that she wondered if Helen had waited until eight o'clock to ring, knowing that someone was usually at the base by that time.

'I'd like to speak to Peter if I could, but if he's off duty then Jack or Nick would do.'

Katie glanced at the wall, where a large whiteboard showed who was doing what and where.

'Peter's on duty; I'll put you through,' she said, then heard a deep voice say,

'Peter's here.'

She spun around in her seat to see him smiling at her from the doorway.

Normal internal turmoil, she decided, diagnosing her reaction dispassionately. She smiled a greeting to show that there was nothing wrong!

'Helen Jensen on the phone,' she said, surprised to see that he was carrying a litre of milk in one hand and a tray in the other.

'Switch it to conference, would you please, Katie? I need my breakfast before I can think in the morning.'

As she switched the call so that Helen's voice could be heard by both of them Peter poured milk into the large glass he'd brought in on the tray, took a ham and cheese croissant from a paper bag and bit into it.

'Go ahead, Helen,' he said, gulping at the milk. 'I'm organised now.'

'It's Carly Simpson's baby,' Helen said, her voice

so clear that she could have been standing in the room with them. 'She's having gastro-oesophageal reflux problems—'

'And Carly's concerned,' Peter finished. He sounded as if he knew Carly Simpson well. She must be a regular at Castleford clinics.

Katie crossed to the patient files, found Carly Simpson's and a separate file for the baby, Therese. She dropped them both on the table beside Peter and received an absent-minded nod.

'Yes,' Helen was saying. 'I keep telling her it's normal for babies to regurgitate small amounts of milk after meals, but I haven't reassured her much.'

'How old is the baby now?'

'Three months,' Helen said. 'I've told her it usually stops between six and nine months, but she's not convinced I'm right and wants me to send her to town and have tests done.'

As Katie watched Peter shook his head and frowned, the food and milk forgotten.

'I hate doing tests on young babies until everything else has been ruled out,' he said. 'They are invasive and uncomfortable. Let's start with basics. Could the vomiting be connected with anything else? Middle ear infection? Some other illness?'

'No temperature, no signs of hernia, nothing physical or viral that I can find. It's also been happening for some time, which usually rules out an infection.'

Katie watched Peter write down the information on the file.

'Is it straight after feeds?' he asked.

'No,' came Helen's reply, and Katie sensed concern in it. 'It's about an hour after feeds, which is usually more indicative of a pathological oesophagitis than physiological, isn't it?'

Peter agreed, still writing, then asked about the texture, mentioning coffee grounds—which puzzled Katie. Helen must have understood.

'Yes, but there's no bile staining,' she explained, 'which should rule out an intestinal obstruction, and no blood.'

Was there a 'yet' hovering behind that sentence? Katie wondered, absorbed, as she always was, in the long-distance discussion of a medical problem.

'I suppose you've suggested reduced feeds, given more frequently?' Peter was tapping his pen against the desk. Was it a mannerism when he was thinking? Had she noticed it before?

'We've been trying that all week,' Helen replied.

'Is the baby thriving? And is she breast- or bottle-fed?'

He was frowning again, Katie noticed, and she guessed that he was trying to picture the infant in his mind to make the hands-off consultation a little easier.

'She was, but the weight gain has stopped—which could be a natural plateau or something more sinister.'

Peter wrote another note, then the pen tapping started again as Helen launched into a long explanation of why Carly had switched to formula feeds.

'It makes it easier for us,' Peter cut in. 'Tell Carly to thicken the formula with a little cornflour. I've got the amounts here somewhere.'

He looked up at Katie, saying, 'There's a fairly recent therapeutics journal with an article on infant reflux somewhere in that pile. It should be near the top. Could you find it?'

He waved his hand towards the book-shelves, then smiled at her. Although she told herself that it was a normal Peter-smile, her stomach did a double twist—

possibly with pike, she thought, remembering diving competitions on the television.

'You know, even with pathological reflux, infants are usually free of symptoms by the time they are two,' he told Helen, while Katie shuffled through magazines. 'What we must watch for now are any indications of respiratory disease caused by the baby aspirating the reflux.'

'I've been checking her chest every time I see her,' Helen assured him.

Katie found the magazine and brought it across to the table. Peter leafed through it, as unaware of her presence as the desk itself was.

'One teaspoon of cornflour to 100 ml of water is the measurement, Helen,' he said. 'It should be cooked in the water, then the formula mixed in later. I'll be in Castleford on Tuesday, but if you're worried in the meantime call in.'

'I'm not worried, Peter,' Helen said briskly, and they heard the click as the link between them was disconnected.

'It's natural the mother would be upset,' Katie said, her heart going out to the unknown woman.

Peter, toying with what must be the unpleasantly cold remnants of his breakfast, dropped the croissant distastefully then looked up at her.

'Of course it is,' he agreed, surprising her with unmistakable empathy. 'But, even when the parents are anxious and urging tests, we should always try conservative measures first. If the thickened feeds don't work, and the baby shows significant failure to thrive, we can introduce a drug. Several have been tried over the years, but Cisapride is the most popular these days.'

She must have reacted visibly, for he grinned at her and said, 'See, even soft-hearted Katie shudders at the thought of putting a three-month-old on drugs!'

'Did I?' she asked, returning his smile—and wondering why he thought of her as 'soft-hearted Katie'. 'I suppose it's the word ''drug'' that hits home. Lay people tend to forget that the panaceas we pop into our systems are actually drugs.'

Peter was finishing the milk, and watching him swallow seemed too intimate a thing to be doing. She turned back to her desk and sat down, willing the phone to ring.

It didn't, so she thought of the baby—to stop herself thinking of Peter—and another question popped into her head. She spun her chair back to face him.

'Would you give a drug before you did tests?'

'After a full examination,' he replied. 'And only then if I was satisfied that there were no signs of obstruction. If there was no significant weight loss I would probably try a drug before tests, but it doesn't always rest with the GP.'

She looked at him, confused by the emphatic statement.

'If the parents are very anxious we can't refuse to refer the infant to a paediatrician for tests,' he explained. 'We can advise, but we can't do more than that. I'll take blood and arrange a full blood count and ferritin measurements on Tuesday because iron deficiency anaemia is suggestive of oesophagitis.

'If the thickened feeds don't help, we'll fly Carly and Therese to town and I'll send the baby for a barium swallow to rule out obstruction. A specialist would order pH monitoring and could arrange a scintiscan. Adult reflux is investigated with an endoscopy, but that is rarely performed on infants.'

Katie shuddered again.

'The thought of it makes me go cold all over. Poor baby!'

Peter pushed aside the remains of his breakfast, then looked up at her.

'And, speaking of babies, how are the ones I foisted on you?'

This is normal colleague-to-colleague conversation, Katie! she told herself, when the teasing smile which accompanied his question did some teasing beneath her ribcage.

'You can have them back any time you like,' she promised him. 'They kept me awake most of the night.'

'Did they?' he murmured in a peculiar voice which made her wonder what else he might be asking. His eyes repeated the question—but what question?

Fortunately the phone rang at that moment. She swung back to face the desk and grabbed the receiver gratefully.

'Yes, Eddie,' she said, and heard Peter murmur,

'I didn't sleep either,' as he left the room.

She wrote down the roster changes that Eddie was dictating, but as she replaced the receiver an emptiness crept over her. She knew that it was because Peter was no longer there—which was stupid, because he was so rarely there why should she miss him?

'Yes, Jack!' She fielded the next call, made a note that he wanted print-outs of the duty rosters to take home overnight and then switched him through to Leonie.

To take her mind off Peter, she was giving some thought to the lack of status attached to being a telephonist, compared to a radio officer, when the radio call came in. She jotted down the particulars, sent a 'Priority One, destination Crane Island,' message on the pager to the pilot on duty and went in search of Peter.

'It's a young diver with the bends, Peter. It happened out on Lomax Reef. They tried to reach the search and rescue helicopter, but it's at a caving accident further north. The patient is one of a group of six divers who went out to Lomax on a fast catamaran. They're heading back to Crane Island—ETA in twenty-five to thirty minutes.'

'Did you page the pilot?' he asked, his beautiful blue eyes intent on her face.

'Priority One call immediately,' she assured him.

'Will you be able to patch the dive boat through to the aircraft radio?'

Katie thought for a moment, then shook her head. 'I could try, but I doubt it. It's a small boat, which does runs between the resort and the outer reef. Its radio would be strong enough to contact the island resort but not much further. I was lucky to pick it up directly.'

Peter considered her words for a moment.

'OK,' he said. 'We'll have to relay. Could you get back on to the dive boat and take down the history of the dive? The hyperbaric staff at the hospital will want the depth and duration the time it took to ascend the timing of the onset of his symptoms any unusual complications and any treatment they have given.'

Katie moved to the side of his desk and picked up a piece of paper on which to write the list.

'Got all that?' he asked, and she nodded.

'Then ask them for a list of symptoms and let me know on the flight. Ask about joint or limb pain, skin rash or itching, fatigue, nausea, visual disturbances, headache, communication and any motor or sensory disturbances.'

He paused again.

'Following all this?'

'Just!' she said, still writing.

'Great! Now—' He stood looking at her—but not

seeing her, she was sure, as he thought through the evacuation flight.

'I'll go without a nurse,' he added slowly.

He looked up suddenly and smiled at her, then seemed to lean forward a little as if he was going to. . .

'I'll get on to the dive boat immediately,' she said quickly, and hurried away.

CHAPTER SIX

PETER followed her, heading for his car, his thoughts
not on the diver with the bends but on the young woman
he'd all but kissed—again! The impulse hadn't arisen
from any conscious thought, yet he'd caught himself
leaning towards her, and in his mind he'd already felt
the coolness of her lips—the lack of heat which had
vanished when the fiery conflagration erupted.

Decompression, recompression. He repeated the
words in his head as he drove to the airport, determined
to forget about that startling finale to Monday night's
visit to Katie's home—and his subsequent perplexity.
After all, a person couldn't suddenly become attracted
to someone they'd known as a friend for years! Could
they? He felt his traitorous body give lie to the thought
and groaned aloud.

Eddie was waiting at the airport, the C200 ready for
take-off.

'It's a diving accident,' he told Eddie as he climbed
on board. 'Katie will radio through more details.'

'Pity we haven't one of those new portable decompression units,' Eddie muttered, and Peter smiled at him.

Air transport for patients with decompression problems was always risky because the altitude of the flight
worsened the patient's condition.

'We can keep our pressure up if you stay low, can't
we?' Peter asked, and received a confirmatory grunt
which was loaded with disapproval.

'You know how Civil Aviation feel about our "staying low", as you so quaintly put it. I put in a request

and they go berserk, then give me twenty reasons why they should deny it. I make it safely back and Leonie chews my ear for the cost of the extra petrol. Maybe I should sell my house and the kids and pay for the Duocom unit myself.'

He was still grumbling quietly when they lifted off.

Peter watched Eddie's skilful handling of controls, and listened as he talked to the tower about his return flight. RFDS planes had priority at the airport and a jumbo jet could be held up while an emergency flight landed, but, as a centre for tourism, the airport also had more than its share of light aircraft buzzing around its skies and these were what worried Eddie when he was forced to undertake a low altitude return flight.

'We're in their space, flying low like this,' he had once explained to Peter.

'Is Peter there, Eddie?'

Katie's voice reminded him that he had problems of his own. He listened while she sketched in details of the accident, then frowned as she listed the patient's symptoms, finishing with paralysis of his legs.

'Those boats should carry oxygen as the very least of emergency equipment,' he muttered frustratedly, knowing that the paralysis would be the result of an arterial gas embolism. How far would it move before they could get the patient into a decompression chamber?

'Tell them to keep him supine, Katie,' he snapped. 'If they've got oxygen on the boat, or have some on the island, tell them to administer it through a face mask at one hundred per cent, six to eight litres per minute. If they have an emergency oxygen tank all they have to do is set the dials and turn on the tap.'

'There's none on the boat, but they are nearly at the island. I'll pass on the message. You could phone the island if you think of anything else.'

She gave him the resort number, sounding crisp and efficient—exactly as she had sounded for the last three years. And why shouldn't she? Nothing had changed.

Then why did he feel annoyed?

He looked out at the jewel-bright sea beneath him— at the dotted islands, so thickly forested that they looked like rich, mossy rocks set in an ornamental pool.

'You coming straight back?' Eddie asked, interrupting any further flights of fancy.

'Yes,' Peter told him. 'I'll get him on board first and do what little I can in the air.'

'What can you do? You can't recompress the poor blighter without the proper chamber.'

'I'm hoping they'll already have him on oxygen,' Peter replied. 'Extra oxygen can create a gradient for eliminating the excess nitrogen. I'll put in an IV line and pump fluid into him. More fluid means more blood to carry the gas out of the arterial system.'

'Well, I suppose they'll be doing whatever they can for the fellow,' Eddie said, as the low buildings of the exclusive resort at Crane Island came into view.

While Eddie circled above the strip, losing altitude before landing, Peter phoned the island, asking the receptionist to pass on the message that they were about to land and would pick up the patient and depart again as quickly as possible.

'He's already there, by the look of the activity,' Eddie said, pointing to a flat-tray truck with a blanket-covered figure clearly visible on it.

'And on oxygen,' Peter acknowledged, peering downward. 'At least that's something.' He glanced at his watch as he felt the plane stop, interested to see how long it would take them to load the patient and be on the move again.

'Five minutes,' Eddie called, as the wheels rolled again. 'Not bad, eh?'

Peter grinned. He was bent over the young man and hadn't given the turn-around time another thought.

While Eddie taxied, he set up an IV line then attached the leads of the vital signs monitor. In spite of the evidence of the mechanical reading, he checked the man's chest with his stethoscope to make doubly certain that there were no symptomatic sounds suggestive of a pneumothorax—as common in decompression accidents as it was in road vehicle injuries.

'Strap in while I take off,' Eddie called, and Peter dropped into the seat across from his patient. He used the time to jot the monitor readings onto the patient file—'BP 140/86, heart rate 116, and respiratory rate 42.'

'OK!'

Peter unstrapped as Eddie's equivalent of the commercial airlines' 'You may now unfasten your seat belts' echoed through the cabin.

He checked his patient again, alert for any sign of seizure activity or deepening shock. The young lad was comatose, a sickly greenish-grey in the cabin light. His pallor was accentuated by a shock of black hair which flopped untidily across his forehead.

Peter continued his examination, testing the lad's reflexes and adding further notes to the file. Once satisfied, he picked up the note that was attached by a huge safety pin to the blanket which covered the young man.

At least, here, someone had known his job. The details of the dive were neatly printed below the patient's name and local address.

'Care of Crane Island Resort—that's a help,' Peter said as he read it. The name, Carlos Solano, told him no more than he'd guessed when he'd examined his patient. Italian or Spanish, he'd decided, and, judging by the name, possibly more Italian? He wasn't certain. If he was resident in Australia the resort would have his home address, and if he was a foreign tourist his passport would be with his belongings at the hotel.

Satisfied that his patient was stable, Peter moved forward to the copilot's seat for touch-down and radioed the base.

'Could you get on to Crane Island Resort, please, Katie,' he said, 'and find out if they have contacted the young man's relatives? Get any information you can from them in case the hospital staff need to speak to someone in his family.'

'I'll get those details for you,' she said, 'but I know the resort has already spoken to the young man's father. He's on the phone to Leonie at the moment, calling from the north of Italy. Extremely calm and controlled but determined to have all the details now, at once, immediately, if you please.'

He could picture her eyes growing stern and her wide mouth turning down at the corners as she parodied the man's demanding tone. He smiled at the image.

'If he's still on the phone tell Leonie to tell him his son will be in the hyperbaric chamber within fifteen minutes, and if he leaves a contact number I'll get the unit doctor to phone him as soon as they've settled on a decompression depth in the chamber and begun treatment.'

'I'll do that now,' she said, and he heard her sign off as Eddie taxied to a halt outside their hangar.

They were watching the ambulance drive their patient away when the next call came through on the mobile phone. It was Katie again, relaying another message.

'There's been a fellow savaged by a wild boar— lacerations to his calf, hand and arm, and badly torn calf muscles. Three men on a shooting trip. They've driven him to Mt Relax Station and the manager phoned us. He's wrapped up the injuries as best he can but the man's lost a lot of blood.'

Peter turned to Eddie.

'How long to Mt Relax?' he asked.

'Forty minutes. We going right away?'

Peter nodded, and watched Eddie head for the office to fax through a flight plan. There were days like this when one call followed hot on the heels of the next— and other days when you waited for calls that never came.

'Tell them we'll be forty minutes,' he said to Katie.

'Do you want a nurse?' she asked. 'Christa's on call and she's here at the base. She could be at the airport in ten minutes.'

He thought for a moment, mentally picturing what he would have to do when he arrived at Mt Relax. Eddie emerged from the hangar, and that decided him.

'No, Eddie and I are still at the airport. Two minutes to grab some gear and we can be on our way,' he replied, talking as he hurried across the tarmac to fill a cool-box with blood products and fluid. 'With blood loss and the subsequent shock that ten minutes might make a difference. There'll be staff at Mt Relax, and Eddie to help if I need a hand.'

He heard her murmured agreement before she said, 'I'll tell Christa. Here's the Mt Relax number. Once you're in the air you'll get them on the mobile net.'

He smiled at her unflappable efficiency. Leonie might be Base Manager but Katie guided them through their airborne adventures, anticipating what would be needed and smoothing the way for them so that they could do their jobs free of petty annoyances or time-consuming co-ordination. That was *one* Katie!

Katie replaced the receiver and relaxed in her chair for a moment. Evacuation calls demanded one hundred per cent concentration, and one hundred per cent called for extra effort on her part these days. Since Monday, in fact!

Leonie appeared in the doorway.

'Mr Solano, the father of the young man who had the diving accident, is flying out from Italy. I've made a booking for him at the bay Hotel. If he rings again, and I'm not here, could you tell him?'

Katie nodded, but her eyes must have asked the question.

Leonie sighed.

'He was worried sick, Katie!' she explained apologetically. 'I had to promise I'd go up and see Carlos for myself, and speak to the doctors.'

'And I suppose you gave him your home number so he could contact you there?' Katie spoke accusingly, but she softened the words with a smile. They were all guilty of caring what happened to their patients; guilty of giving up private time to follow through on cases that had particular significance to them.

'I try to keep it to a nine-to-five job,' Leonie said helplessly. 'Or eight-to-four, in my case!'

Katie nodded. Leonie had begun work at the base when her children were too young to be left unsupervised after school, and her hours still revolved around being at home when they were.

'You don't have much success,' she teased, knowing that Leonie made herself available to speak to relatives of their patients at any time, especially the families of overseas or interstate tourists who were hospitalised far from their homes.

'I think how anxious I'd be if it was Mitchell or Caroline in hospital on the other side of the world.'

'I know,' Katie said softly as Leonie walked away. She watched her go, wondering again about the quiet, efficient woman who ran the base. She was still young—under forty, Katie was certain—and extremely attractive with her grey eyes and streaky, ash-blonde hair. Perhaps Jack and she. . .

Katie brought her thoughts back into focus with a little shake of her head, feeling the new length of her hair swish around her ears. Indulging in romantic speculation—even about Jack and Leonie—was extraordinary enough to shock her back to normality.

She lifted the receiver, silencing the sharp ring of the phone.

'ETA at Mt Relax in ten minutes, Katie,' Peter's voice said but, judging by her reaction, she wasn't quite back to normality! 'I've let them know, and will phone you with an ETA at Rainbow Bay when we're airborne again.'

She opened her mouth to point out that Eddie—or whoever was piloting the flight—usually radioed their ETAs, but then decided that she wouldn't call attention to Peter's departure from routine.

She contented herself with a carefully casual, 'Thanks, Peter,' and was about to disconnect when he added,

'And don't forget it's late-night shopping this evening. I'll be back in time to go to Logan's with you.'

And what will Eddie think about that remark! she wondered, as she replaced the receiver. What Eddie knew Susan also knew, and Susan loved to embroider even the vaguest of hints into romantic patterns. Would Susan realise that Peter was only advising her on clothes? That he always did this for quest contestants? Or would she read more into it?

Katie shivered. The ramifications of their names

being linked in Susan's mind were too horrible to contemplate. Peter would probably assume that she'd said something to someone on the staff—made false assumptions. . .! The shiver became a shudder, but then she heard an echo of his words, 'I'll be back. . .with you!' and the heat she tried to deny banished the shivers and shudders, surging through her body and betraying the orders of her mind.

So this was desire! This was what she had known was missing from her relationship with Richard—the thing she had been unable to put into words. Did it always spring up so quickly, spreading through the tissues like an out-of-control bush-fire? Could it happen without reason to suppose that the desire was in any way returned? Apart from that one unexpected kiss, Peter had shown no new or unusual interest in her; done nothing to fan the flames which had leapt to life within her.

Yet what she felt could not be denied, and she was forced to face the fact that the self she'd imagined to be too practical, too in-control, for passion didn't exist.

'Katie!'

She spun around to see Christa in the doorway.

'Daydreaming?' Christa teased.

'Who, me?' Katie countered, defending her old practical, common-sense image. 'Sleeping, maybe, but never daydreaming!'

Christa chuckled.

'I came to tell you I've a home for those puppies.'

Conscience-stricken, Katie glanced down at her watch. She'd promised faithfully to go home in her lunch-hour and feed the brood.

'All four of them?'

'All four,' Christa confirmed. 'A friend is training dogs as companions for elderly people who live on their own, and for retirement villages. He says people prefer homely, mixed-breed dogs to thoroughbreds.'

It was Katie's turn to laugh.

'Well, he couldn't get anything more homely or mixed than those puppies,' she agreed. 'Would he like me to keep them until they're eating real food?'

But as she asked the question, she remembered another difficulty. Her parents were going away that afternoon and she would have to find someone else to feed them during the day. She was relieved when Christa shook her head.

'If it's OK with you he'll pick them up from your place today. He says the sooner he starts handling them the better,' she replied.

'Companion dogs need a lot of physical contact so they grow up accustomed to pats and cuddles.'

'Like people,' Katie said, and won a smile.

She turned back to her desk, writing notes against the quickly logged calls she'd taken during the morning. Base records were a protection against argument later on, and a guide to the future needs of each particular area. In the six years Katie had worked at the base she had seen the number of evacuation flights double, mainly because of an increase in travellers and tourists through, and within, their area.

Where once an emergency flight would usually collect a stockman injured in a fall, or a country woman whose baby was arriving before its time, nowadays the majority of evacuations dealt with car accidents— people travelling too quickly over rough roads which were unfamiliar to them.

But a man savaged by a wild boar? That was new!

Peter crouched in the back of the dusty vehicle and looked at the wounds. Ideally, the lacerations should be flushed clean and stitched immediately, but there were deep puncture wounds among them—perfect breeding places for infection. He swabbed the patient's uninjured forearm and sank a wide-bore catheter into place.

'Get hold of someone at the base,' he said to Eddie. 'Ask them to phone the hospital and request a surgeon be standing by when we bring the chap in. Tell them there's been significant damage to the right calf muscle and blood vessel lacerations in the right forearm and right leg. That way, they'll know who to get.'

He was working as he spoke, starting fluid, wrapping the arm wounds in medicated gauze to prevent any further infection entering on the journey to the hospital. Blood still seeped from the leg wound, and the faint distal pulse confirmed that a clot had formed to slow the bleeding. Repairing the torn blood vessels was work for a microsurgeon, and speed became essential.

He covered the leg with moist dressings, and walked beside the stretcher as willing hands carried the man from the back of the four-wheel-drive vehicle to the plane. Holding the fluid bag, he watched the man's chest rise and fall, his breathing unassisted but through a mask—a high oxygen mix.

Someone outside pushed the door closed and he heard Eddie snap the lock.

'Let's go,' Peter said, clipping the infusion bag onto the rack above the stretcher, then reaching across his patient to ensure that the strong steel clips had latched into place. The plane accelerated across the gravel strip, and he strapped himself into his seat and reached for a patient file. The man's name, Bernie Shaw, and an address in the southern city of Melbourne had been handed to him earlier.

'That makes it easier,' he said to his unresponsive patient as he copied the name and address onto the wide form. He ran down the list of initial observations, thinking how often he had written those classic signs of shock. Respirations shallow, pulse 100 or higher, skin cool, pale and clammy, capillary refill two seconds plus.

'You can unstrap,' Eddie called, and Peter realised that the floor had levelled out. Time to go back to work!

Using the IV port he was feeding both analgesic and antibiotic drugs into his patient. He knew that the crystalloid fluid would reduce the level of shock until the patient's blood could be typed and matched. Aware of the danger of sepsis, he drew up a double dose of tetanus immunoglobulin and injected it slowly into the man's left thigh, then began his secondary examination.

'ETA ten minutes,' Eddie called.

Peter left his patient and walked through to the cockpit to look out over the Bay. It was a place of unique beauty, like an imagined paradise, with its blue waters and scattering of green-clad islands, creamy sands and hidden coral reefs.

'Best sight in the world, isn't it?' Eddie said, surprising Peter with the genuine warmth in his voice.

'It is,' Peter agreed. 'But I wonder if, because it's so familiar to us, we take it for granted?'

'I don't,' Eddie said firmly, but Peter had walked back to strap himself into his seat, wondering if that was true of other things besides nature's beauty.

He phoned Katie from the mobile on his way from the airport.

'Do you want to go home before we go shopping?' he asked, then listened to the long silence his question had provoked.

'Yes!' she said at last, wishing that he'd asked another question—one with a simple yes or no answer like, Do you still want to go? 'I can't try on clothes all sticky from a day at work.'

What a stupid thing to say, she thought, only half

listening to Peter's arrangements. His other girl-friends—the smooth, sophisticated blondes she'd seen dangling from his arm like trophies—would never get sticky, she was sure.

Other girlfriends?

You're not in that category, Katie! she reminded herself, and agreed when he suggested a time to collect her.

The call completed, she bent again over the paper-work she was trying to complete. At least the dampening effect of 'other girlfriends' had squashed the tiny spurt of joy that hearing his voice had triggered.

She was sitting on the front step when he drove noisily up her quiet street. The puppies had gone off to their new home, and her parents were heading south to their conference. Waiting for Peter out here seemed safer than waiting inside. Her home was her refuge and, even after two casual visits, a suggestion of his presence remained.

'Locked out?' he asked as she hurried out to the gate.

'Sad, isn't it?' she countered, unable to hide the smile his physical appearance invoked.

He had obviously been home to shower and change. Now he seemed to gleam in the late afternoon light—golden hair burnished by the last rays of the setting sun; freshly shaven skin shining with health, and his blue eyes—

Her mind went blank as those blue eyes caught her questing gaze, and held it for an infinitesimal moment.

Her chest thudded with a sudden awareness of him—a physical knowing as real as if their bodies were touching so closely that no air could pass between them.

'Straight to Logan's or will we grab a bite to eat first?' he asked, and she wondered if she had imagined a strange huskiness in his vibrant voice. 'My experience tells me shopping can be both tiring and time-consuming. Perhaps food. . .?'

She eased the air from her constricted lungs. Two words, 'my experience', were all it had taken to break the spell—to land her feet firmly back on the ground.

'Well, it's my shout this time,' she said, hoping that such practicality would show him that she thought of him as no more than a helpful friend.

He opened the car door for her and glanced quizzically into her face.

'Five-star restaurant?' he said hopefully.

'McDonald's or the snack bar next to Logan's,' she retorted, ducking past him and slipping quickly into her seat to avoid a helpful hand on her elbow. 'Take your pick!'

'The snack bar it is, then,' he said as he joined her and started the engine. 'But it is not your turn, Miss Independence! I promised you a dinner when you spent the night holding my hand—metaphorically speaking—that night on Coorawalla.'

What could she say?

'Did I ever thank you?' he asked, and something in the gravity of his voice made her turn and look at him.

He was waiting for a gap in the traffic on the main road, and his attention was concentrated on the steady flow. His profile, with its rounded forehead, straight, sculpted nose and strong chin, reminded her of old medallions. But the beautiful, curving lips softened the image. Finely ridged around the edges, they were full and shapely—lips that smiled easily and kissed like. . .

He glanced towards her and she turned hurriedly away, trying to remember why she had looked at him in the first place. Had he asked her something?

They drove on in silence.

'I'll park here and we can walk through the arcade,'

he suggested and she nodded, too absorbed in remarshalling all her protective forces to speak at that moment.

She watched as he pulled the waterproof cover over the car seats and snapped it into place. His hands moved with a sureness which mesmerised her.

'There's an Italian bistro in the arcade. Shall we try that instead of the snack bar?'

Be sensible, Katie, her mind warned.

'OK,' she agreed lightly, 'but it's still my turn to pay.'

She walked away from treacherous thoughts of strong hands biting into her skin, kneading her flesh.

There's no future in dreams, she reminded herself.

'So, have you heard how your diving accident patient is doing?' she asked as they settled at the table. Talking about work should block out the insidious appeal of this man who was trying to be her friend.

'I phoned the hospital before I left home,' Peter told her, handing her a bright cardboard sheet with crayoned scrawl and illustrations proclaiming the dishes of the day. 'They put him in the chamber at four atm.'

He looked enquiringly at her, one eyebrow lifted.

'No, I have no idea what atm is,' she admitted, smiling slightly at his quizzical expression.

'It's an atmosphere of pressure,' he explained, then paused while the waitress took their orders. 'I won't go into how scientists figured out the weight of one square inch of air in a column up to the atmosphere and worked out all the figures, but it comes down to the fact that a diver at thirty-three feet is experiencing an ambient pressure of one atm.'

Katie hoped it looked as if she was listening intelligently but, as Peter's hands drew out his explanation in invisible lines on the table-cloth, her mind had slipped from control once again and was imagining delights that shocked her.

'So, the hyperbaric chamber can be set at different atmospheres,' he continued. 'Young Carlos regained movement in his feet in the chamber at four atm, but the doctor will probably order two more treatments at three atm. He's quite certain the young man will recover completely.'

'His father will be relieved,' Katie muttered, pleased that she'd dragged herself back to the present in time to catch the end of the conversation.

Their meals arrived and Katie looked down at the plate in front of her, wondering what on earth it was. She remembered ordering something, selecting a number absent-mindedly from the list.

'It's a pizzetta with olives, anchovies, capers, sun-dried tomatoes, bocconcini and basil,' Peter murmured, and she looked up to see him smiling at her, his eyes dancing with glee.

'Did I order it?' she asked, unable to believe that she could have chosen something so exotic.

'You did,' his said, the gravity in his voice belied by the teasing merriment in his eyes. 'If you don't want it we could swap.'

She looked across at his plate and saw a crisp pile of calamari, golden brown, heat spiralling off it.

'I'll eat it,' she said reluctantly, wondering if he thought her boringly unsophisticated. 'It looks—interesting?'

He grinned across the table at her.

'Interesting enough to share,' he suggested, and reached out to take her plate. Half the pizzetta was urged carefully onto his side plate, then he used a fork and spoon to fill the space on her plate with calamari. She reached out to retrieve her plate and their fingers touched. The plate fell, landing, with all food intact, on top of a small tray of condiments.

'I'm sorry,' Katie muttered, acutely aware that her cheeks were flaming.

Peter looked at her, his eyes dark and faintly hooded. He glanced away for a moment, looking first at her hand—scrabbling to retrieve the plate—then at his own—fingers drumming on the table-cloth. Then his head lifted again, and she saw the faintest line of a frown between his dark, heavy brows.

His gaze travelled slowly over her face, so deliberately that he imagined she could feel it, then returned to meet her eyes again.

'I don't think I am,' he said, very slowly. Then he repeated the obscure remark.

'I don't think I am.'

CHAPTER SEVEN

'ORDEAL by shopping!' Katie muttered as she pulled off a rose-coloured evening gown, which she had known would make her look like an over-dressed turnip, and reached for a dark green silk creation which had caught her eye on her previous abortive expedition.

'It's strapless,' she had objected when Peter had drawn it from the rack and added it to the pile over the saleswoman's arms.

'So?' he had enquired, his gaze never moving away from her face.

She had turned away to hide the colour in her cheeks as her mind had added the words he hadn't said—the 'You've plenty to keep it up' the shop assistant had told her the last time she was in Logan's.

'Well, it might be too bare at country dances!' she had retorted, and had stamped off into the dressing-room.

It was the last ball-gown in her size in Logan's, and she handled the soft, slithery folds gingerly—a bomb which might explode at any minute!

'Do you need a hand?' the saleswoman called.

'No!' she yelped.

It was bad enough that she was surveying all the pale bare flesh the gown revealed without having that bossy stranger see it. Maybe if she had a tan she wouldn't look so—naked? Creamy skin, paler against the dark silk, seemed to dominate her reflected self—creamy skin and the deep cleft between her breasts!

She grabbed the top of the dress and tugged at it,

trying to pull it up—to cover the expanse of lush body so provocatively revealed.

'Come out and show us, Katie.'

Peter's voice—not demanding but showing the first edge of impatience, which was natural enough in a man who had spent the last two hours in a woman's domain.

'It doesn't fit,' she told him yet, as she uttered the untruth, she turned side on and lifted her hands to hold the side wings of hair high up on her head.

Hardly daring to breathe, she surveyed the stranger.

She looks beautiful, she thought, awed by the image, yet not accepting that it was herself.

'Are you decent?' he asked, his voice closer—just outside the cubicle curtain.

'I don't think so,' she said doubtfully, still caught in a dream that it might have been she who had looked so beautiful. She dropped her hands and turned the other way, then the curtain twitched aside and she heard the catch in Peter's breathing before his face came into focus beyond the stranger in the mirror.

'It's stunning,' he said quietly but his eyes were on her face, not on the dress. 'Absolutely stunning.'

'But it's too—' She resisted the urge to lift her hands and cover the visible areas of breast. If he could stand in a dressing-cubicle of a women's boutique and behave as nonchalantly as he would in the public bar of the local, then surely she could show similar ease.

'Daring?' he suggested. His eyes, a deeper blue than normal, slanted a quick look downwards, then returned to focus on her face once more.

'The other quest contestants will be wearing similar gowns,' he told her, his voice rasping against her ears. 'You must remember that people in the country are no less fashion-conscious than their city cousins.'

She tilted her head to one side, still watching him in the mirror.

'But there's a "but" in your voice. I can hear it.'

She felt a sick, contrary disappointment. True, her first sight of herself in what she now thought of as 'the dress' had been shocking, but she would have liked Peter to like her in it; liked him to have seen that fleeting glimpse of beauty in the office 'plain Jane'.

He hesitated a moment longer and she found that she didn't want to wait for his reply.

'I've got a ball-gown at home that will do,' she said, hiding the silly pain under briskness. She turned to pull the curtain across, wanting to get out of the disastrous gown——to get back to normal!

He didn't step away so her movement brought her up against him, the pale, swelling breasts thrust against his cotton shirt. She felt his glancing appraisal, felt heat sweep through her body and then, with little regard for his still-hobbling state, she thrust him backwards and snapped the curtain shut, blinking against a smarting tightness in her eyes.

'We'll pack the clothes you've chosen and send them to your home in the morning,' the saleswoman told her when she emerged, clad in her own linen shorts and shirt. 'Peter said he'd meet you at the car.'

Peter said? Did he shop here often enough for the saleswoman to know his name?

'I don't want the green silk,' Katie told the woman, although the denial caused her real pain.

He was leaning against the car——one hip hitched onto the bonnet——when she emerged into the car park, and looking not towards the arcade but out to where the traffic flowed along the town's main street.

'I'm sorry I've kept you waiting,' she said to his

broad, unyielding back. 'You could have gone. I'd have found my own way home.'

He turned and stared at her, frowning as if he'd forgotten who she was.

'Did you take that dress?'

Abrupt! Demanding!

'No!' she snapped, disconcerted by his tone. 'I decided it wasn't my style.'

He had unclipped the car cover while he waited and she opened the passenger door and slid into the seat, anxious to get home; to get away from him—from the strange mood that had been generated between them.

They drove back to her house without speaking, while guilt that she might somehow have upset him itched along her nerves. He had been kind enough to help her choose suitable clothes—a task she would have found impossible without his help. Besides, there was the future to think about—their day-to-day contact at the base.

How difficult would that be now that this wall had suddenly risen up between them, casting its long shadow on what had begun as an amusing and enjoyable interlude?

'Would you like a cup of coffee?'

The invitation arose from her desire to make amends, yet it trembled fearfully on her lips.

'I'd enjoy that,' he said, his voice deep and full of shadows. 'I found your parents charming.'

Oh, dear!

'They're away!' She blurted out the words, not knowing if that would make him change his mind. Or make him think that she was inviting him to. . .

Oh, hell!

He braked and the car stopped opposite her front gate.

'I'd still like coffee, Katie,' he said, turning to study

her face in the light from the street-lamp. 'If you think that's wise.'

She frowned at him, puzzled by his choice of words.

'A cup of coffee alone in the house with you won't make me a fallen woman either,' she said stoutly, remembering this was her opportunity to get things back into balance between them—back into normal, worka-day balance!

She heard him chuckle as she clambered out of the low-slung seat, and knew that he was following her up the path. Her feet hesitated for an instant as an inexplic-able doubt fluttered like a chill breeze in her heart and then she walked on, putting herself into the hands of fate.

She could feel his presence behind her while she unlocked the door; heard his footsteps follow her into the hall. Then her feet faltered and her name, a gentle, barely whispered, 'Katie,' fell about her ears and she turned in the darkness—turned slowly and deliberately, knowing that there would be no escape; knowing that she would be turning straight into his arms.

Her lips were cool, as he'd remembered them, but they were the coolness of ice that could burn as badly as any fire. Don't do this! To Katie—to yourself! an inner voice commanded, but his body was beyond the control of inner voices. It was determined to taste again the passion he must surely have imagined; to banish from his mind the notion that something unbelievable had sparked between them.

Skin so soft that his hands slid across it without directives from his brain. Don't think of soft skin! A kiss, that's all, the voice told him. One swift, experimental kiss.

Then her lips parted beneath his and he tasted her special sweetness, felt her tongue entwine with his and her teeth press against his lips. Was her body throbbing that he could feel the pulse of it against his chest, or was his own so out of control that his heart was pounding? The darkness of desire swept up to cloud all thought, and his hands pressed her full, rich body hard against his torso.

The heat would burn right through her at any moment, Katie knew. It was rampaging in her veins and thundering in the centre of her being, consuming pride, and common sense, and conscience, and leaving only more desire in its wake.

Peter's hands cradled her hips, pressing the aching hub of her body against the hardness of his. She moved against him, not knowing what she wanted of him but aware that he could sweep the flames into some final conflagration beyond anything she had ever experienced or imagined.

One hand slid across her breast. Stabbing pain! Shooting pleasure! She moaned against his mouth.

'This is leading to only one place,' he muttered, words muffled as lips moved on lips, neither of them willing to give up the desperate, delectable contact.

In a dim recess of her brain she knew that the words were a signal—that it was time to push him away as she had done once before—but her hands were busy exploring the feel of muscle-clad bone in his shoulders, and her mouth was too busy with kisses to speak.

Then kisses weren't enough, and the urgency flaring through their bodies found expression in fingers that slid, teasingly possessive, across skin which tingled at the touch.

Then Peter straightened, and the warm night air brushed her tender lips. He held her with one arm around her shoulders—close, but not as close as her body would have liked.

'This is wrong, Katie,' he whispered in the darkness, and one finger traced her profile—forehead, nose— and, oh, so gently, teased across her lips. 'For one thing, I'm supposed to be looking after you, and whipping you off to bed is hardly honouring my responsibilities as a courtier to the Queen.'

'I'm nearly twenty-four, Peter,' she protested as his fingers burnt a path along her neck, then plucked absent-mindedly at one hardened nipple—accentuating pain, accelerating pleasure. 'I'm not an inexperienced school-girl who needs looking after!'

She heard the words echo through her family home, and blushed in the darkness. She might as well have said, Take me to bed!

'Not a schoolgirl at all,' he murmured, touching his lips to hers again. 'Schoolgirls don't light these kind of fires.'

She felt his heart beating as the kiss deepened, but then he growled, deep in his throat, and pulled away again.

'This is madness, Katie,' he said hoarsely. 'And I'm to blame for starting something that cannot be finished.'

Was it 'kiss intoxication' or the release of three years' pent-up emotion that forged the next words? Afterwards she wondered, but now all she knew was that someone was saying, 'We could finish it,' in a tight, faint voice that definitely wasn't Peter's.

His hands gripped her shoulders and he gave her a little shake.

'We can't, Katie, and that's that!' he stated harshly. 'In spite of what you might think, I certainly didn't come prepared to seduce you. So, quite apart from other complications in my life which make things difficult, I doubt if you're the kind of girl who keeps a handful of condoms in her bedside drawer. One thing even schoolgirls should have learnt by now is never, never, never to have unprotected sex until the health of both parties has been checked.'

His fingers were biting into her flesh, as if he could impress his words physically through her skin. She should have been shocked by what he was saying, but two words—'other complications'—had sent her spinning into such despair that consideration of safe sex was the last thing on her mind.

'Then perhaps you'd better go,' she said, amazed at how cool and controlled she sounded when her heart was beating out a plea for him to stay, and those two definitive words were clashing like cymbals in her head.

'Katie!' Not a name but more a deep-throated groan, wrung reluctantly from a man whose control had come close to being snatched away.

'Now, Peter!' she said, her jaw aching with the determination it took to hold back a wail of despair.

He turned and walked away, his footsteps hammering across the wooden verandah like nails hammering into a coffin.

She lay awake most of the night, brief snatches of conversation replaying endlessly in her head. At seven o'clock she considered ringing Leonie and saying that she was sick, but that was the coward's way out.

She stayed in bed a little longer, although even that was torture because she kept imagining what might have been! She tried to visualise the roster—maybe Peter was on a full-day clinic flight.

No good! He was on call all week—she'd known that all along.

But 'on call' didn't mean you had to be at the base. He was well within his rights to be on call at home, or anywhere he wanted to be within a certain distance of the airport. Maybe he wouldn't come in!

Having decided this, she hurried to get ready. The thought of food made her feel sick, so she skipped breakfast and drove down to the base.

'Peter and Jane were called out to an accident near Wooli,' the woman on duty at the answering service told her when she phoned to say that she was switching calls back to the base. 'Two young jackaroos heading back to work at Stretton Park on a motorbike. Ran off the road and the pillion passenger was able to go for help, but it took him two hours to walk the six kilometres to the station. The call came through at three-thirty-six.'

Katie made a note of it, although the answering service kept their own log of calls. She thought about the young man who had walked through the darkness; imagined his pain and despair as he pushed on towards the sleeping homestead. It was preferable to thinking about other things!

'Good morning, Katie.'

Leonie popped her head into the radio room.

'Greg Jamieson, the president of the Rotary Club, phoned me at home last night. He wondered if you would be able to go along to their meeting this evening.'

'Today's Friday,' Katie said suspiciously, not ready to cope with the social ordeal that lay ahead of her. 'Rotary meets the first Tuesday of the month.'

And don't ask me how I know, she added silently. In all the turmoil of being chosen as the base contestant, she'd managed to overlook the fact that Richard was a Rotarian.

'. . .as the wives will be present as well, they thought it would be a good opportunity for you to meet them. Peter's invited too, of course, unless there's someone you'd prefer to take you.'

'I don't need to be "taken",' she said bluntly. 'Peter and Jane have had a three-thirty call-out so even if he isn't called out again he'll probably appreciate an early night. I'll be all right on my own.'

'Good for you.' Leonie smiled. 'The dinner's at the Bay Hotel; drinks beforehand in the Oriental Room at seven. Semi-formal, I'd say—the men in suits, the women in cocktail dresses. Did your shopping spree yield up something like that?'

Tactful Leonie! Katie returned her smile.

'There's what Peter called a "useful little black number",' she replied, and silently congratulated herself on saying his name aloud without a stutter.

'Just the thing,' Leonie assured her. She hesitated in the doorway for a moment longer, then added, 'Enjoy it all, Katie, won't you?'

It sounded like a plea. Katie looked at the slim, attractive blonde framed in the doorway and wondered again about Leonie's life.

'I will,' she promised and, as she said the words, she knew that she would make them come true. It was as if last night's brief experience had liberated her in some way.

She worked steadily through the day, determined to finish early and go home for a few hours' sleep before she had to go out. Before she had to get dressed up to go out! she amended, because for this final month the Rotary Club was going to have the best darned candidate it had ever had. She was going to make them proud of her, and she was going to enjoy herself!

The silent pledge was put aside, but not forgotten, as she answered consultation calls, putting them through to Nick who was on duty at the base.

'Katie, I'd like to see you tonight. I want to talk to you.'

The sound of Peter's voice—deep-toned and edgy—after a day of business calls sent her mind into chaos. Now was the time to tell him about the Rotary dinner, she realised, but the words wouldn't come out.

'I'm busy tonight,' she said. Tonight was Friday. Hope and suspicion battled for supremacy. If there was anything stronger than a purely physical attraction on his side surely he would suggest that they meet tomorrow night—Saturday night. And would she say yes if he did?

'Could I see you when you've finished being busy?' he asked quietly, and her stomach churned. Why would he want to see her late at night—except to kiss her senseless, then back away from her again with excuses she didn't want to hear? Or would he come—prepared?

'No, Peter,' she said and was about to hang up when she heard him speaking again.

'Then I'll come up to the base right now,' he said angrily. 'I'll see you before you start being "busy". Damn it, Katie, I want to talk to you, not seduce you.'

And it was he who hung up.

She sat and looked at the phone, as startled as if it had bitten her. Then panic set in. She didn't want to talk to Peter—and she particularly didn't want to talk here at work. Not when he was angry, and his voice would reverberate through the old house. Not when other people were likely to come in and wonder what was going on.

'This is Bill Wilson at "Wetherby", Katie.' The call brought her mind slamming back to the job. 'I'm radioing from my truck. You wouldn't believe it but the helicopter mustering pilot has come down in the same place as that light plane crashed a few months back. The rotor must have clipped the top of an old, burnt out tree at the top of the ridge! No blood but she could have a back injury, I'd say. Will you send someone out?'

'She?' she questioned while she checked the roster. With only one patient to retrieve, a clinic plane could sometimes be diverted. No good! The only clinic plane was coming in from the north and 'Wetherby' was south-west.

'About a third of the muster pilots are women these days,' Bill explained.

'Good for them,' she said. 'I can't divert a plane so we'll send one. Peter's on call. I'll get on to him, and get back to you on the radio. What frequency are you using in the truck?'

Bill had stated his call sign and frequency when he had called up on the emergency band, but asking him to repeat it was a confirmation that she had it right.

'5145 kilohertz, Katie,' he replied, and signed off.

She paged the pilot then dialled the on-call mobile number. A phone rang loudly behind her.

'I'm here, Katie,' Peter's voice said—but not in her ear.

She turned slowly, the protesting squeak of her office chair echoing her sentiments exactly.

He stood there, tall and solid, his arms hanging loosely by his sides and his face unsmiling—somehow giving the impression that he was inviting her inspection. Inspection? Her eyes were more likely to absorb him than inspect him—seeing through clothes to the body beneath, the body which had fired hers to such—

'A muster helicopter has come down at "Wetherby".' She threw the words at him, fighting off the betraying weakness seeping through her veins. 'No blood, suspected back injuries. Bill's at the site and I can get him on the radio. Do you want to speak to him now or should I patch him through to you on the plane?'

He moved a step closer, and she panicked.

'There's no time to talk now, Peter,' she stuttered. 'I have to call Jane.'

'Then I won't hold you up with a radio call. Patch Bill through to me on the plane,' he said coldly.

He watched her turn back to her desk, and shook his head. He was thirty-one years old and couldn't remember when he'd last acted as foolishly as he had acted last night. One kiss was excusable! But his body's strong reaction to that kiss—a reaction that had shocked and embarrassed him—should have been enough to make him keep his hands off her.

And then to mumble on about 'safe sex' like an elderly school teacher while his body ached to hold her, take her, make her his—if only for a few ecstatic moments.

And Katie? How did she feel? He stared at her back and thought about enigmas.

She was holding herself stiffly and, more than anything, he wanted to cross to the desk and knead the tension from her shoulders. He couldn't bear to think of her hurting! Perhaps when she finished talking—

'Peter's on his way to the airport,' he heard her say, and knew that she wouldn't turn around again. He walked out of the radio room, heading for his car, and another emergency evacuation—another day, another call. This was his chosen career, he reminded himself, a life that demanded all his energy and commitment. He tried to summon up the edicts of his father which he had accepted without question for so long; tried to remember the arguments which had seemed so logical and believable.

He shook his head and started the car, then drove towards the airport, trying to picture the injuries he might find when he reached his patient at 'Wetherby'—

trying to ignore a voice which was asking questions about excuses!

The young woman had been lifted out of the helicopter and driven to the airstrip.

'She regained consciousness and could move her fingers and toes,' Bill explained, 'so we thought we'd bring her to you.'

Peter climbed onto the truck and knelt to examine her, feeling her skull, neck, limbs and torso.

'Maybe you were lucky,' he said and the young woman, who had introduced herself as Brenda, grinned at him.

'Maybe I'm a cat, and have eight lives to go,' she suggested.

'I wouldn't count on it,' he told her. 'Think of this as a lucky escape which has given you a second chance at life!'

Second chance! Would there be a second chance for him with Katie? Did he want one? Would he ask?

Bill drew him aside while Jane started a drip.

'Hope we haven't got you out on a false alarm,' Bill said quietly, 'but she was out like a light when I radioed the base, and the chopper had dropped like a stone—I was sure there'd be bad injuries.'

'Don't apologise,' Peter reassured him, pleased to have his mind diverted back to practical matters. 'No one likes being underworked more than doctors. We're delighted, not upset, if we come out on a call and find things better than we expected. All too often, the opposite applies—'

'And you find your patient dead,' Bill finished sympathetically. 'I understand.'

They watched as three young stockman, acting under

Jane's orders, lifted Brenda carefully onto a scoop stretcher.

'We'll take her back to the hospital for the night, at least. They can check her out for any internal injuries, and will want to keep her under observation after the concussion.'

They secured the stretcher into place on the plane, and Michael taxied to the end of the strip to turn for take-off.

'Do you want to sit up front?' Jane asked.

'No, I'll do the patient file and chat to Brenda,' he responded, and watched her walk forward to the copilot's seat.

Strapped into a seat across the aisle from his patient, Peter glanced at his watch. It was six o'clock. Back in town by seven.

'Got a date?' Brenda asked, smiling teasingly at him.

'No,' he said. 'She's busy!'

He must have put an extra emphasis on the final word for the young woman to shake her head so sympathetically.

'Nice-looking guy like you would never be lonely. You'll soon find someone else to console you,' she said.

'I don't know if I want to.' The words came out without his thinking of them, dragged from some part of his subconscious mind that he hadn't known existed.

That's ridiculous! he decided.

'Of course you want to,' Brenda joked. 'What are you? Twenty-eight? Twenty-nine? Far too young for a gorgeous chap like you to tie yourself to one woman for life!'

Her declaration shocked him, mainly because he suspected that it verbalised his own unacknowledged sentiments and the conceit behind such a thought was sickening. Could that be why he'd been using his erratic work hours and his father's belief that doctors shouldn't marry young as excuses to avoid long-term relationships? Because he enjoyed his bachelor image? Enjoyed having no ties?

He thought about it for a moment.

No, he decided, it had been far more complex than that. Something to do with not questioning that particular advice, because he would then have had to question other things his father had decreed! But now the questioning had begun. . .?

He turned his attention back to Brenda, who was watching him with a little smile twitching the corners of her lips.

'I'm older than I look,' she said, 'and I've been around. I can pick a playboy a mile away. But someone's rocked you, haven't they? Made you doubt all the excuses you've used for not settling down?'

Her questions disconcerted him, and again he turned to work to fend them off.

'Who's the doctor and who's the patient here?' he demanded, pulling out a file and fixing it to a clipboard. He settled it on his knee, thumbed the point out on his pen, turned to his patient and said, 'Now, full name and address.'

First and foremost he was a doctor, he reminded himself. That was one commitment he did have! And Jenny! Two commitments!

CHAPTER EIGHT

KATIE smiled and talked and laughed as if social occasions in the large function room at the five-star Bay Hotel were an everyday occurrence in her life. She hadn't needed her father's words to impress on her the importance of giving as much as she could to the task she had undertaken. A sense of duty was an integral part of her character, bred into her and heightened by her upbringing.

'Well, is it the haircut or the excitement of being a Queen of the Outback contestant that has put such a sparkle in your eyes?'

She'd known that Richard would eventually make his way to her side. He'd done it unobtrusively, nodding to her across the room while they enjoyed pre-dinner drinks and raising his glass to her in a swift, silent toast when their eyes met during the meal.

Now the evening was ending, she had thanked her hosts and Richard had materialised by her side.

'It's probably the dress,' she told him, looking up into his pleasant, open face and wishing, yet again, that things could have been different between them. He was so loving, so caring—so generous in every way. 'Logan's have fitted me out for every occasion.'

'It's very smart,' he agreed, but she saw another message in his eyes.

'May I drive you home?' he asked, and she shook her head.

'I've got my car,' she explained, while her mind marvelled at how one man's eyes could make you feel uncomfortable while another's set your blood on fire.

'Then I'll walk you to it, Katie,' he said, and took her arm.

Peter, standing with Leonie and Alessandro Solano on the far side of the hotel lobby, watched them walk past. So, she'd told the truth! She *was* busy tonight. Very busy, by the attentive look that dark-haired chap was giving her!

'Doesn't Katie look lovely?' Leonie exclaimed as she, too, caught sight of the pair. 'And back with Richard. How nice!'

Back with Richard? Back with *Richard*?

Peter tried it both ways in his head, but neither eased the black rage that had erupted so unexpectedly within his body.

He watched her look up at the stranger and laugh as she walked through the door.

Richard—whose phone number she knew by heart!

Beside him, Leonie was explaining to the foreign visitor that Katie was the radio operator at the base.

'This base you talk of all the time,' Alessandro said in his smooth, accented voice. 'I will be permitted to see it? You will show me one day when I am not with Carlos at the hospital?'

'I must be off,' Peter said abruptly, although he definitely wasn't going to obey an urge to drive past Katie's place to see if a strange car was parked outside. 'I had an early call this morning, and have to catch up on some sleep.'

Leonie smiled her goodnight and the visitor hardly seemed to notice his departure, being engrossed in Leonie's explanation of how the RFDS operated. Or engrossed by the sparkle in Leonie's eyes?

Peter frowned as he walked away. Leonie sparkling?

He was imagining things! The episode with Katie had unsettled him.

He felt his muscles contract—stirring, stiffening. An episode, that's all, he repeated to himself to combat the reaction.

He remembered the feel of her in that dark hall, and the faint smell of her hair lingered in his senses.

The memory did nothing to cool his body. He had a day off tomorrow. Maybe what he needed was a drink.

He walked into the bar and studied the array of bottles behind the barman's head, then walked out again. Alcohol wasn't the answer. He had to talk to Katie; to make things comfortable between them again; explain what he could. He would phone her in the morning. After all, with the projected trip to Coorawalla and the Queen activities, they would be spending plenty of time together.

And that thought didn't cool his body either!

Katie rolled out of bed, surprised that she'd slept so soundly. It was eight o'clock and she was the volunteer on duty at the animal refuge this weekend. Fortunately, seeing Richard last night had reminded her that she, too, had 'other complications' in her life. She dressed quickly, ate a hurried breakfast, threw enough food to keep her alive over the weekend into a large basket and left.

The refuge raised sufficient funds each year to pay staff during the week, but with wages doubled or trebled by overtime rates over weekends it made sense to use volunteers. Once a month she slept over in the tiny flat attached to their animal hospital, feeding the sick or injured native birds and animals which were brought to the sanctuary.

'As well as our usual strays and recuperating accident

victims, we've all the survivors of the cyclone,' the warden greeted her. 'Five orphaned possums, a bandicoot, three fledgling grass whistling ducks and an immature koala who, believe it or not, must have fallen out of tree. It's got a broken leg.'

Katie followed the warden around the enclosures, listening while she explained who was eating what.

'I'll manage,' she said, as the woman departed for her own house across the road from the centre.

'I know you will,' her friend replied.

Katie watched her go, relieved to be alone in this quiet place of healing, yet glad that she would be too busy to brood.

This was normality for her—weekends at the refuge, time spent playing and coaching sport. It was a normality that suited her, that she enjoyed. All she had to do was settle back into it!

Peter made it easier and harder.

He breezed into the office on Monday morning, teased Sally—which was normal—made an obscure remark about rich foreign gentlemen to Leonie—which wasn't—said 'Hi,' to the staff gathered in the radio room—Susan, Jack, Nick and Katie—then, with a casual, 'Can we meet tomorrow about Coorawalla, Jack?' he was gone, flying with Michael and Christa to a one-day fun day at a property in the far north of the cape run by the School of Distance Education.

'This is Alessandro Solano, Katie.'

Katie turned from her desk, where she was doodling on a piece of paper and thinking unproductive thoughts.

She turned around and smiled at the stranger.

'Carlos's father?'

The stranger smiled and nodded. White teeth sparkled behind tanned skin and, with his dark hair now predominantly silver, he looked more like a film star than anyone's father.

'Could you explain about our radio net to him, and the School of Distance Education operations?' Leonie asked.

Katie was puzzled, but she nodded her agreement and waved the visitor to a seat beside her. Leonie knew as much about the radio as she did, and more about everything else the base did. Why wasn't she explaining?

'With half my staff going off to Coorawalla I've a great deal of work to do.' Leonie answered the unspoken question, but didn't explain her agitation. She was definitely uneasy—flushed and a bit fidgety.

'So, please call me Alex; it is easier. You have worked here how long?'

It was the first of a thousand questions. The man had a mind like blotting paper, absorbing facts as quickly as Katie could supply them. He sat patiently when Katie answered either the phone or radio calls, but she knew that all the details were being filed away in his formidable brain.

'Now, Peter was telling me of a trip north he was taking today. He explained it was a school day of some kind.'

'The School of Distance Education runs field days in different areas, and all the families who are within travelling distance of the chosen place converge there.'

'Is it educational?' Alex asked, then waited while Katie switched a consultation through to Jack.

'It's more a fun day for the kids. They get a chance to play games with other children and do craft activities.'

'And your plane is there in case of accidents?'

'Partly,' Katie explained, 'but our staff also use the day to speak to the adults who brought their children along. Families can discuss any concerns they have. It might be about the use of something in the medicine chest which is supplied to all isolated families. Or the doctor might give them practical sessions—preparing a syringe and injecting water into oranges, for instance.'

'So it is a chance for the medical people to see families in a non-medical situation.'

It was a statement, not a question, and Katie turned to look more closely at her interrogator.

'You don't miss much, do you?' she remarked, softening the words with a smile. 'It is exactly that. Families who live in isolation experience all the same fears and ambitions, tensions and strife that other families have. But they have fewer support systems in place, and no close neighbours, family or friends who might notice when things are going wrong.'

'You talk of problems in marriages—in relation-ships—of adolescents wanting to break away, of alcohol abuse and the subsequent possibilities of other abuses?'

'All those things,' Katie agreed sadly. 'Jack believes, and all the medical staff agree, that our presence at social occasions is important. We are there in case we're needed, of course, but it's also an opportunity for the staff to see people interacting with each other and with their families.'

'All part of your mantle of care,' the man said softly, echoing words that had been used within the Service for more than sixty years. 'I read all I could find about it. It's a long flight from Italy,' he explained. 'My organ-isation has a medical library which includes wide information on medical services as well as other, more scientific details.'

Intrigued by the words 'my organisation', she was

about to ask questions of her own when the phone interrupted them again.

'Katie, check your quest schedule. Tomorrow is a Castleford clinic day—I think it might be the fund-raising card day. If I'm right, ask Jack to make the meeting Wednesday. He's on call this week so, with any luck, we can cover all we need to talk about in between his consultations and call-outs.'

Her heart, which had leapt uncontrollably at the sound of Peter's voice, settled back to its normal rhythm. He'd sounded so calm and impersonal that he could have been speaking to his dentist—if someone with a perfect smile had a dentist!

That's how you wanted it, she reminded herself. Normality, remember?

But not so much normality that she'd totally forgotten the functions arranged for this week!

'Excuse me,' she said to Alex, rifling through her drawer to find the quest information she'd thrust in there last week. 'There's this Queen thing on. I'm taking over from the base entrant, and I'm forgetting appointments before I've even begun!'

The older man smiled.

'I am interrupting your work too much, but I would like to know more of "this Queen thing". Perhaps Leonie will explain. . .?'

Did Leonie want him back? Katie sighed. She had too much bothering her right now to worry about Leonie.

'I'm sure she would,' she told him briskly, sacrificing her boss with only a momentary qualm.

She found the schedule and realised that Peter had remembered correctly. She was due to play cards at Castleford tomorrow. She hoped that they could play Fish and Snap because that was where her card knowledge began and ended.

She pressed Jack's extension and explained the problem with the proposed meeting.

'Wednesday should do,' he agreed. 'Get back on to Peter and tell him that. And you'd better warn him—and Susan and Eddie—that I'll be giving you all gamma globulin injections at the same time.'

'Thanks!' Katie retorted. 'I'll look forward to it.'

She replaced the receiver and paused for a moment, subconsciously preparing her body for the impact of Peter's voice on the phone. She dialled, heard it and spoke quickly, hoping that she sounded businesslike—not panicky.

'—Wednesday's fine with Jack,' she finished and hung up again, puzzled by his reception of her message.

When he'd spoken to her earlier he had sounded abrupt, but hearing his voice had been a shock and she could have been mistaken. This second conversation had not been unexpected, and the abruptness had taken on the undertones of anger.

Anger? What had he to be angry about? If anyone should have been angry, it was her—or was it she? Oh, bother grammatical correctness! Bother everything. And damn and blast as well. While growing up, she'd heard worse swear words but, as a minister's daughter, she'd taken pains to keep them out of her vocabulary so now, when she needed a bit of strength and force to express her frustration, she was at a loss!

She thought about teeth grinding and realised that she didn't know how to do that either.

A phone call saved her from any further demonstrations of pique, and when the radio crackled to life she welcomed the diversion and turned her mind thankfully back to work matters.

A call from Joan at Wyrangi hospital, soon after Nick had left on an evac flight, caused a flurry of activity.

A man had come in with all the signs of anaphylactic shock—apparently unaware that he was allergic to shellfish when he'd decided to sample Wyrangi's famous prawns.

Jack had been in the radio room when Joan phoned, and had taken the call at Katie's desk. She sat and listened to his side of the conversation.

'He was conscious when you gave him epinephrine intramuscularly?'

Joan must have agreed.

'And what about laryngeal oedema?' Pause. 'You've got a tube down, and have him on oxygen—good! Get an IV catheter into him, Joan. He could need more epinephrine fast, and it will also give you a chance to balance his fluids. Have the defibrillator standing by. I'll get a doctor to you as soon as possible and we'll bring him back here. From the sound of things he could need more life support than Wyrangi can provide.'

Katie could imagine Joan's relief. She pulled forward the map she'd opened while Jack was talking.

'Peter's here,' she said, pointing to the property where the school gathering was being held and measuring the distance between the two places with her fingertips. 'It would only be about twenty minutes' flying time from Wyrangi.'

'Can we get him on the phone?' Jack asked.

'We can indeed,' she told him, and pushed the phone towards him. She would have to talk to Peter again some time—like tomorrow on a trip to Castleford—but she didn't have to hurry into anything.

Tomorrow came soon enough. Katie woke with a feeling of doom on her chest like a large rock. A late-afternoon call from a lone sailor on a yacht had kept her and Jack in the radio room until midnight. The man had injured his arm and shoulder when he'd fallen against the mast in a sudden wave surge. The reception had been so poor that it had taken hours for symptoms to be relayed, and step-by-step advice sent back across the airwaves.

A sense of the man's loneliness had swept over her as his voice came and went from the room, and she had needed all her skill to find him again and all her strength to encourage him to repeat each direction Jack gave— to ensure that their transmission was reaching him.

When Jack was finally satisfied that the man's arm and shoulder had been immobilised she had stayed on, calling for other boats which might be in the area and giving the location of the injured man, until she'd found a fisherman who had seen the yacht earlier and would track it down and tow it into port.

The successful conclusion should have buoyed her up, she told herself, staring up at her ceiling and wondering how she could avoid the day that lay ahead of her.

'Phone for you, Katie!'

Her mother's voice reminded her that she should get up and greet her parents. They had returned from their conference yesterday, but she'd been too late home to see them.

She forced herself out of bed, and walked through to her father's study to take the call.

'It's Leonie, Katie. Jack's arranged for Alex Solano to go to Castleford with you. Would you mind collecting him from the hotel on your way to the airport?'

Was Carlos's father someone important? she wondered vaguely, making her way to the kitchen and greeting her parents. The Service often took visiting doctors or people with a special interest out on clinic flights. But parents of patients?

By the time they reached the airport she was pleased that she had his company. He was a charming man, and so fascinated by their work that it would have been impossible to dislike him.

She was chuckling over a chance remark when he opened her car door for her and reached out a hand to help her stand. With a silent insistence he took the small bag she carried with her.

'You are staying overnight?' he asked and she shook her head, explaining as she led him across the apron to the waiting plane.

'I think today is only cards, but I brought casual clothes as well in case they include a horse.'

'A horse?' He turned and gazed at her in amazement and, smiling broadly, she told him about photo sessions and horses.

But the smile faded when they turned towards the plane again and she remembered Peter's promise to hold all horses. Sadness came with an icy sweep when she realised that they could never again share that easy companionship.

Peter's face was just as unsmiling. She looked up, unaware of his presence, and saw him frowning down at her and Alex from the cabin doorway.

'Have you met Alex?' she asked him, uneasily aware of his anger and more uneasily aware of how his body was affecting hers.

'We had dinner together on Friday night,' Peter said, clipping off each word with a razor-like sharpness. 'Alex!'

He inclined his head towards the other man.

'A passenger, have we?'

Katie turned with relief to see Allysha walk through from the cockpit. She hadn't thought to ask who was flying them.

She watched as Peter introduced Alex to the two women, then the visitor was swept into the copilot's seat by Allysha and Jane dropped into the seat immediately behind the pilot. Katie, after a moment's hesitation, sat behind Jane and felt Peter move into the next position in the single row.

Her skin knew that he was there and she squirmed in her seat, ashamedly aware that she wanted to feel his fingers on her shoulders; to have him touch her, however lightly—to be her friend again, if nothing else!

But they had moved past the simple pleasure that was friendship and, to Katie, it was as if she had walked out of a field of bright spring flowers into a morass of sticky, clinging, churned-up mud.

'The card game is at the hotel. We'll drop you there on our way to the hospital where we hold our clinic.'

The information was offered coolly—smooth words touching her ears, not lingering fingers touching her skin!

'We usually finish the clinic in time to get down there and join in a late lunch. Do you want me to come in and introduce you?'

'I'll look after you,' he'd promised, when she'd agreed to enter the quest.

'I think I can manage to find my way through the door and blurt out my name,' she retorted, even more coldly.

Silence.

She peered through the window and watched the newly green landscape, blessed by the cyclonic rains, unfurl itself beneath them. She saw the dots of the cattle property buildings and brown sweeps of rivers filled with their seasonal rains, bringing new life to the country through which they flowed.

'Katie. . .?'

The word hung in the air, begging her to turn around,

but she knew that she didn't want a pretence of friendship—didn't want to hear any more excuses or explanations. Yet the word had not been angry! It had been soft, with an undertone of hopefulness!

'It's good to see the country after rain,' she said as casually as she could manage with throbbing pulse and paralysed lungs.

More silence, then, 'Yes,' he answered—crisply— not defeated, but perhaps angry again.

'We're coming down. I presume you lot are buckled up,' Allysha called to them.

Katie checked her seat belt automatically and then looked out of the window again, anxious to see the place that she felt she knew already.

'It's the original one-pub town,' Jane said, closing the book which had occupied her throughout the flight. 'But it does a good lunch, doesn't it, Peter?'

Peter mumbled some reply as the wheels touched down and the plane's momentum began to slow.

Definitely angry again, Katie decided, and stayed in her seat while the others went through what was obviously a ritual, stacking the bags of equipment they would need on the floor inside the cabin door. By the time they came to a standstill the medical crew was ready to go.

Alex came through from the cockpit, eyes widening at the sight of all the gear.

'I may come with you? Sit in on your clinic?' he said to Peter.

'Yes, grab a bag,' he said, more sharply than Katie had ever heard him speak. 'Everyone lends a hand out here.'

I wonder if that remark is directed towards me? she thought, and made sure that she was carrying her own bag and another from the pile when she stepped down onto the runway.

The second bag was unexpectedly heavy, but she clung determinedly to it as she followed the others across to a waiting minivan.

Peter led the way, and when he'd piled the gear he had carried into the back of the vehicle he started back towards the plane.

'That's too heavy for you,' he snapped, grabbing at the medical equipment.

She refused to release it so they stood, each tugging at the handles of the case.

'I can carry it,' she said stubbornly. 'You said yourself that everyone had to lend a hand.'

'Don't be ridiculous, Katie,' he answered, equally stubborn. 'It's the last bag and I'll carry it.'

He gave an extra tug and his fingers moved against hers—the fingers she had longed to feel on her skin.

Staggered by her thoughts, she dropped her hold and the bag slipped to the ground between them.

'Now look what you've done,' he muttered, but he'd lifted his head to berate her and his eyes caught hers—and held.

She recognised the ache of longing because she knew exactly what it felt like. All around them silence—high blue sky and stretching open plains—and between them a burning, pulsing, fiery hunger!

She bent to lift the case, breaking the unspoken communion. A physical appetite, she reminded herself, that's all it is.

He snatched it away from her and marched off, and she followed, hurrying now—not wanting to keep the others waiting any longer.

Castleford's women had turned out in force, and Katie was welcomed with warm outback friendliness.

They were not demonstrative people, these bush women, but their sweet smiles were genuine and their soft-voiced conversation drew her into their lives.

Bert Grimes, the hospital cook, was organising the card games.

'We'll make more money after lunch when the men join in,' one woman told her.

'When the men join in?' she repeated, and the woman explained.

'Most of our husbands see it as a good day to come to town as well. They go to the machinery store, or the bank, or do whatever business they have to do, then they all come back here for lunch—especially when they know Bert's OK and doing the cooking.'

Katie hid the smile that twitched at her lips. She'd heard stories of Bert's alcoholic benders, which were becoming legends of the outback, but these people protected their own and she didn't want this new friend to think that she was laughing at Bert.

'I've heard he's a great cook,' she said, then tried to concentrate on what the woman on the other side was telling her about the rules of canasta.

She was still trying to understand the card game when Bert called the lunch-break.

'The doc's here now and the nurses, so we'd best feed them in case they get called away.'

Katie looked up and saw Peter introducing Alex to a group of men who hovered at the back of the room. He turned sharply, as if aware of her regard, and she blushed and looked away. Other things were impinging on her consciousness, including a delicious aroma of baked meats.

'While Bert serves dinner I'd like to introduce the medical team,' Helen Jensen, matron at Castleford's small hospital, called out. 'Not that most of you need introductions.'

'And introduce our candidate to the men,' someone reminded her, while Jane looked around, found Katie in the crowd and beckoned her forward.

The introductions were completed, and the crowd was filing out to a huge marquee erected behind the hotel when a chilling cry stopped the flow.

Katie sensed the confusion was behind her somewhere, and pushed herself back against a doorway to allow Helen and Peter to get through to whoever was in trouble.

'If you could all go on through to the refreshment tent,' Jane called out.

Katie, knowing the milling crowd would need a leader, said, 'Come on,' and led the way out of the hotel.

She was as curious and concerned as the rest of the visitors, but knew that the medical staff could do more for their patient without a horde of onlookers.

She was shown to a table at one end of the tent, but didn't sit down. Something in the wailing terror of that cry told her that it was a medical emergency, and in that case their plane might soon be taking off. She glanced at her watch and saw that it was already two o'clock.

The crowd had settled down, news of what was happening being whispered between them but the thought of lunch growing in importance in their minds. Satisfied that she could do no more there, Katie excused herself, slipped away from the table and crossed to where Bert was supervising the distribution of the meals.

'It's a shame to miss out on such a spread,' she said, smiling at the battered-looking old man, 'but if the doctor decides his patient should go straight to town we'll all have to go. I don't suppose I could make up a few sandwiches for the crew to eat on the plane?'

Bert beamed at her.

'I'll do them for you,' he promised. 'And I've got something special as well. I was making pastry for the tarts so I threw a few of my special pies into the oven. I'll do some sandwiches and pop in some pies as well. Enough to feed—how many?'

Katie counted.

'Five, with the pilot.' Allysha would have brought her own lunch because she'd intended staying out at the airfield, but they could hardly sit around eating Bert's special pies in front of her without offering her one! He smiled again and nodded, then whisked away towards the hotel.

'Peter sent me to find you.'

She turned to see Alex coming towards her.

'Are we leaving?' she asked.

'As soon as the transport they use as an ambulance arrives,' he explained. 'It seems that while everyone else in the district came to town the man who drives the ambulance went fishing—in the ambulance.'

He shook his head as if such a story was totally unbelievable.

'It probably isn't a real ambulance,' Katie said, trying to explain the vagaries of transport in the bush.

'That's what Peter said,' Alex told her, taking her by the arm in a courtly fashion and leading her back towards the hotel. 'It makes no more sense when repeated.'

She chuckled at his confusion.

Peter was waiting on the wide verandah, a scowl of impatience marring his good looks. As they drew closer the scowl seemed to deepen, and Katie fancied that it encompassed Alex as well as herself. In fact, it seemed to be directed more towards Alex than herself.

'Come on, Katie,' he said harshly, 'we can't be waiting around while you socialise.'

I'm supposed to be here to socialise, she wanted to remind him, but she bit back the retort and smiled sweetly at him.

'So the ambulance is here already?' she asked, determined not to be cowed by his attitude.

'Well, no—it's not!' he grumbled. 'But I want us all ready to go the moment it arrives.'

'I'm sure we will be,' she assured him, and added another smile that cost an enormous mental effort. 'Excuse me a moment. I'll be right back.'

Did she hear a muttered remark about '. . .women!' or did she imagine it?

CHAPTER NINE

KATIE found her way to the kitchen, where Bert had a cardboard box packed with goodies for them.

'Thanks, Bert, you're a dear,' she said, and dropped a kiss on his wrinkled cheek.

'Now, you come back one day and stay longer,' he said gruffly. 'And get one of the men to carry the box. Pretty girl like you shouldn't be carrying things.'

He hurried back towards the tent to organise desserts for the guests, and Katie left the kitchen. No one had ever called her a pretty girl before. She knew that she could look attractive at times, but 'pretty' was something she'd never considered. Pretty was for petite girls like Allysha, not well-built females like herself.

'You look pleased with yourself,' Jane remarked when she emerged into the foyer again. 'And you're just in time. The truck they pretend is an ambulance is here, and Peter was about to do another little rant and rave about irresponsible women.'

'Then he won't get one of Bert's pies,' Katie said, refusing to let his moody behaviour spoil her pleasure in the day.

'Katie, you're a genius,' Jane cried, taking the box while Katie picked up her bag. 'I didn't give food a thought, but I know from bitter experience that the moment we're all back on the plane my stomach would have reminded me I'd missed lunch.'

'You sit up front with Alex. Jane and I will sit in the back with the patient,' Peter ordered when they emerged from the hotel.

'I'll take the box, Jane,' Katie said, retrieving her burden so that Jane had her hands free to help if she was needed.

As they drove towards the airstrip Alex explained in a low voice that the patient was a young woman expecting her first child.

'It is too early for it to be born,' he said. 'Only thirty weeks. That's why Peter is flying her straight to hospital.'

Some time during the morning Katie had realised that Alex must be a doctor, to be invited along to the clinic and included in the consultation with the patient.

'But if it decides it's coming early there's nothing anyone can do, is there?' she asked, fearful for the young woman and her unborn child.

Alex smiled at her, and she was warmed by a gentleness in his expression.

'There is much we can do,' he explained. 'First we give her an injection of something called betamethasone. It is a product my chemical company also produces, but Peter used a brand made here in Australia.'

'And will that stop the contractions?' Katie asked. They were at the airport now and their silent driver, no doubt upset that his day's fishing had been interrupted, had left the cabin to help Peter carry the stretcher to the plane.

'Unfortunately not,' Alex said. 'It is a corticosteroid that will help the infant's immature lungs develop and prevent respiratory distress if the labour goes ahead.'

'An injection can do that?' Katie breathed, awed by the thought of nature being assisted in such a momentous way.

'Two injections, twelve hours apart,' Alex corrected, carrying the box up into the plane for her. 'If the doctors at the hospital can hold off delivery for twenty-four hours while the betamethasone works, the infant has a much better chance of survival.'

They climbed into the plane and Katie settled in the rear, knowing that Jane and Peter would want to sit close to their patient. Alex dropped into the seat in front of her.

'What shall I do with your box?' He turned in his seat to ask the question and Katie grinned at him.

'Hold onto it until we're in the air,' she told him. 'It might not be what you're used to at the Bay Hotel, but that's lunch.'

He laughed delightedly, and the rich, joyful sound filled the cabin.

Peter looked up sharply from his patient, but the young woman was also smiling so he could hardly condemn the noise.

'Happy back there, are you?' he said and Alex, unaware of any sarcasm, thanked him for his concern!

'And we have lunch,' Alex added, holding the box aloft.

Katie saw Peter look beyond Alex to herself, saw him shake his head and part his lips in a tiny, rueful smile.

Was that an apology for his impatience? she wondered, then hardened her heart against him lest he creep in under her guard again.

'So, while we go up I will tell you what else we can do for the young woman.' Alex had turned in his seat and was looking enquiringly at her. 'You are interested? Yes?'

'Yes, I am,' Katie told him.

'Well, we can also try to stop the contractions with salbutamol. That is what Peter is dripping into her veins now.'

'I thought salbutamol was connected with Ventolin

inhalers—with asthmatic conditions,' Katie said, trying to piece together her limited knowledge.

Alex beamed at her, like a teacher rewarding a bright student with a smile.

'You are correct. It works for asthma because it is a relaxant, and eases the constriction of the tiny tubes in the lungs of asthma sufferers. When we use it for obstetrics it relaxes the muscles in the uterus and, hopefully, stops or lessens the contractions.'

'OK, Katie, where's this food you promised?'

Jane interrupted the medical discussion and Katie looked down, surprised to see the cabin floor level again.

'Alex has it. Could we put the box on a spare seat and then everyone could help themselves?' she suggested. 'I think Bert packed pies and sandwiches.'

'I'll see what Allysha wants,' Jane said, and disappeared towards the cockpit.

'And I will try a great Australian pie. Even in Italy I have heard of this tradition,' Alex announced, reaching forward to drop the box onto the empty seat in front of his.

It developed into a happy, airborne picnic. Bert had packed cans of soft drink and bottles of juice, as well as food. Jane sat in front of the food-seat and passed food either forwards or backwards—the help-yourself idea vetoed because Allysha wanted her passengers either in or close to their seats.

For a short time Katie forgot the shadow Peter had cast across her life, and revelled in the special 'togetherness' that bound all RFDS flight crews into formidable working units.

An ambulance was waiting for the plane, delighting Katie as she saw what actually happened with evacuation flights.

'Usually I'm sitting at my desk at the base, imagining all of this,' she told Alex, who was watching the operation with equal interest.

'But your part in it is as important as that of the medical staff,' Alex assured her. 'It is the co-ordination of the Service that fascinates me.'

'I can drop Alex back at his hotel.' Peter's voice, raised over the noise of the departing ambulance, broke into their conversation. 'It's on my way.'

Katie felt a wave of heat sweep into her cheeks. Peter's clipped words—his increasingly antagonistic attitude—confused her.

'It's no trouble for me to take him,' she argued.

Alex looked at her and then back at Peter, who was standing twelve feet away—his foot tapping impatiently.

'Maybe Peter wants to discuss the patient while we drive back to the hotel,' Alex said apologetically.

'Maybe!' Katie echoed drily, not believing the excuse for one minute. She held out her hand. 'Goodbye, Alex,' she said, battling to regain her composure. 'I hope your son continues to improve and you can enjoy a holiday together before you return to Italy.'

He took her hand and held it while he said, 'He will get better—we know that now—and I intend to stay and see more of your beautiful country, so we will meet again.'

He lifted her hand and dropped a courtly kiss on the back of it. Katie smiled her appreciation of the gesture. He was a true gentleman.

She looked up as he walked over to join Peter, and caught the anger etched on Peter's face. Now what was upsetting him? she wondered. His patient was safely *en route* to the hospital. He'd got his own way over who drove Alex to the hotel, and he was still annoyed!

She hurried towards her car, telling herself that Peter's thoughts and feelings were no concern of hers. But she couldn't make herself believe it. The love she'd felt for Peter for so long had conditioned her to feel his disappointments, as well as his triumphs.

'The "love", Katie?'

She asked the question aloud, unable to believe that she'd finally given a name to the 'thing' she'd had for Peter. What had originally been an attraction to the handsome man with the light, teasing manner had changed recently. Was it because she'd discovered the depth of compassion and kindness that his laughing façade kept hidden?

She unlocked her car and climbed in.

Or was she fooling herself, and trying to legitimatise her physical attraction for him with the excuse of love?

She shrugged away the unanswerable questions and drove back to work where she spent the remainder of the afternoon in the store cupboard, working out which radios to take to Coorawalla.

Coorawalla! The name squirmed within her, its associations with Peter too recent to avoid. But looking at the radios—from the oldest version with its bicycle pedals to the latest mini-marvels—reminded her how much she loved her work. Could she condemn Peter if the 'other complication' was his career? But you didn't take careers out on Saturday nights! her mind argued.

'I thought I'd find you here.' Leonie appeared in the doorway. 'Jack's brought the Coorawalla trip forward. The army people are pulling out on Saturday, and he wants Peter and Susan over there to check on the hospital building before the extra manpower leaves. They'll go tomorrow.'

'Tomorrow?' Katie stuttered, knowing that she wasn't yet prepared to face a week away with Peter.

'You don't have to go,' Leonie told her. 'The fellow in charge is willing to leave his radio operator for as long as our crew is on the island.'

Leonie considered her for a moment, then added, 'In fact, it might work out better this way. Nick's doing an extra two-night trip to Wyrangi, and Nelly Gervase is keen to meet the "new candidate". You could fly up there with Nick in the morning, meet the people and show the flag, and still be back for the contestant dinner on Saturday night.'

Contestant dinner on Saturday night? She'd managed to forget all about that one!

Yet a foolish part of her had wanted to go to the tropical island with the magical name—Coorawalla— and to go there with Peter.

'I'll go to Wyrangi, and be back for the dinner,' she told Leonie, smiling brightly to hide her disappointment. 'They certainly won't need two radio operators on the island.'

'Seven-thirty at the airport,' Leonie said. 'You're lucky—they usually depart at dawn, but they're skipping the mining camps and leaving later because they're taking young Benny and his mother back to join the *Esmerelda*. Get off home now and pack your pretty new clothes.'

She left but drove to netball, not home. She would let the other members of the team know that her appearances would be more erratic than usual. And arrange for someone to take over her juniors for the next few weeks.

'Peter phoned you at about six o'clock. He mentioned dinner, but I said we didn't expect you home until late on Tuesdays.' Her father greeted her with the information when she finally arrived home—tired, hot and sweaty—at ten-thirty.

'It was probably about the change of plans with

Coorawalla. Leonie explained it all to me before I left the office. I'm off to Wyrangi in the morning, and will be back Friday.'

And he'll be in Coorawalla for a whole week! With any luck, we can continue to miss each other like this until all this silliness has worn off, she decided.

But why had he rung, when he'd treated her like a first-class nuisance all day? She took herself off to bed, feeling thoroughly disgruntled—the prospect of a trip to new and exciting outposts dimmed by a simple phone call.

Katie flew back from Wyrangi filled with well-being. It had been as enjoyable and relaxing as a holiday. Nelly Gervase had treated her like a real queen, not just a fill-in contestant in a small quest. She had arranged outings during the day, and fun-filled evenings at the hotel. They were impromptu functions. There were lizard races in the bar, the lizards pampered pets—as cared for and sleekly groomed as greyhounds. And fishing contests—with men from the mines flying in to fish through the night and weigh in their catches the following morning.

As she had watched the members of the small local community part with their money, she had understood what Leonie had meant about the quest being a chance for people to show their appreciation of the Service— and to have fun at the same time.

'Well, did you enjoy it all?' Nick asked her as they unloaded the plane on Friday evening.

'Enormously,' she said, and realised how true that was. She had even managed to forget about Peter—for most of the time. Only when Nick and Allysha were with her, arm in arm or hand in hand, had her resolve faltered, and when Jane had kissed her fiancé long and hard at the airport earlier in the evening Katie's body had ached for a man's arms to hold her close. But apart from that!

She drove home, tired but content, knowing that the break had given her the strength to finally put Peter right out of her thoughts. She might even go out with Richard again.

Her parents were out—not unusual when she considered the projects her father took under his wing—and the letter was propped on her dressing-table. She sank onto the stool and opened it.

'You are a hard girl to catch,' it began, and she knew, without looking at the signature, that it was from Peter. 'I should be—' sitting? '—with you, explaining all of this, Katie,' it continued, 'but as I write you are heading for—' the town names were easy to guess '—Wyrangi, and I will be leaving shortly for Coorawalla.'

The writing was as difficult to read as most doctors', she thought, her heart jostling against her ribs as she tried to make out the words. Strong, and firm and sloping nicely to the right, the writing looked good but was practically illegible. Piecing it together with some difficulty, she came up with,

'For a long time I have used the excuse of my—' career? '—to avoid long-term relationships—' she could almost hear him saying it '—probably because of family—' Was the next word 'influence' or 'circumstance'? Wouldn't 'circumstance' be longer? She frowned over the letter, then realised that the next bit was easier.

As far as she could tell, the letter went on to explain how his mother had died, and told of his father's remorse. 'He said he had used her, Katie. Had taken her youth and drained it away, letting her be mistress and housekeeper, mother to his children and social hostess, but never giving back the love she deserved because he was always too busy, too committed to his "career". He had always thought there would be time later, he said, but, of course, that time never came.'

She put the letter down and sighed, pleased that she'd been able to make that much sense of it. She could understand his reluctance to repeat his father's mistake, but surely his knowledge should work the other way? Wouldn't knowing a trap was there help a person avoid it? She shook her head.

'Doctors should marry late, he—' a string of unfathomable words followed, then '—happy to take it as an eleventh commandment, never questioning the theory or asking how late, never—' 'questioning again', was it? '—anything until very recently—'

He must have started writing more slowly now, for suddenly she could read each word.

'—then again on Monday evening when I teasingly kissed you goodnight and felt something I have never felt before. Is that something worth pursuing, Katie? I think it might be, but it's up to you to decide—and up to you to set the pace.'

The writing deteriorated again here and she thought that it probably said something about telling him when he returned on Wednesday. Then it improved again and she shivered as she read on.

'Perhaps it should be a slow and steady exploration, not that wild explosion of the senses that shook us both the other night. That way, maybe the other complications will have time to sort themselves out and I—'

An hour's hard work had given her that much, and she read the final phrase of indeterminate scrawl over and over again without any luck. She thought she deciphered 'understanding' but nothing either side of it to make any sense. But wasn't what she had already read enough to send her pulse rate sky-rocketing?

Wasn't he saying that he loved her? Or might grow to love her if she gave him the opportunity? Should she ignore the shadowy 'complications' he mentioned? The thing that would need 'understanding'?

Her heartbeats steadied. She couldn't ignore them. He said that it was up to her to decide and, much as her heart might urge her to ignore the warning, her head knew that she could not take even the first tentative step into a relationship with Peter unless she knew exactly where she stood.

She looked at the letter again. Were the words she couldn't understand actually the explanation she needed? No luck! They remained as indecipherable as ever, but she looked up and smiled at her reflection in the mirror. She would ask him and then they could. . .

Begin a slow and steady exploration? Was such a thing possible between them? Already, thinking about him had sent her body temperature out of control and the corners of her lips kept twitching upward in a silly little smile.

And she had to wait until Wednesday before he'd be back! Should she write to him? Maybe he'd phone.

She took the teasing thoughts and shivery excitement with her to bed, and slept blissfully through the night.

Still charged by the excitement of the letter, she sailed through the 'contestant get-together' the next evening. Speaking for fifteen minutes on the work she loved proved easy, and the other young women were friendly and welcoming.

'You're positively sparkling tonight,' Leonie told her and Katie, who had glimpsed her boss in the crowd a little earlier—smiling at the handsome Alex Solano— smiled herself and returned the compliment.

Sparkling—that's exactly how she felt. Even thoughts of Peter's 'complication' couldn't mar her excitement. Once they had talked about it they could work together to resolve it.

She was driving home when she saw the car—small, red and fast—turn into the drive-through lane of the local pizza parlour! Definitely Peter's!

Her heart leapt—he'd come home early!

How could he—from Coorawalla? her brain argued.

Maybe he'd lent the car to someone? She continued driving homeward, but more slowly now as possibilities flashed through her mind.

Lending his beloved sports car seemed unlikely!

Then she realised what was a far more likely scenario. The car had been stolen! Peter would have driven one of the bigger base cars to the airport because of all the gear they were taking. He'd left his car at his house, and some kids were joyriding in it.

Certain that this had happened, Katie turned her own car back towards the pizza parlour, fuming at the thieves' effrontery in actually driving in for a snack. She saw the flash of red outside the servery window—they were still waiting for their order.

Should she drive in front of them and confront them with their crime? What if it wasn't kids—if Peter had lent the car to a friend?

She turned her own anonymous little Corolla around and stopped on the road close to where the car would exit. She would wait and see who was in it before phoning the police or following the miscreants.

He was laughing as he passed her, his face turned towards the woman who was trying to feed him a slice of pizza while he drove, and, although she couldn't hear it, the laughter rang in her head—clear and somehow triumphant!

Peter's laugh was so familiar that she didn't need to hear it again.

Work kept her busy. With only two doctors operating from the base and regular clinic flights continuing, she had to juggle consultation calls—often patching them through to Jack or Nick to handle while they flew between clinics. The letter which had brought such hope lay in pieces in the bottom of her waste-paper basket, the final sentence now gallingly obvious.

'—will be free,' it said. Free of the smiling blonde who fed him pizza? Her long hair had streamed behind her as the car had accelerated away and, to Katie, it had looked like a flag of triumph.

An incidental conversation with Leonie had revealed that Peter had flown back to the Bay with the army force on Saturday, and had returned to Coorawalla on a chartered plane with Alex and Carlos Solano on Sunday evening.

'Alex is a doctor, but he stopped practising to take over the family's chemical plant when his father died,' Leonie explained. 'He has a large scientific laboratory, and is interested in the MVE outbreak.'

Katie knew that she should have been as pleased and excited as Leonie that someone was willing to take scientific studies of the virus further, and perhaps eventually develop a vaccine. But it had made it too convenient for Peter—who had written 'when I return on Wednesday'—to slip back to the Bay and see his 'complication'.

'Are you there, base?'

Unmistakably Peter! The one voice she had hoped not to hear this week.

'I'm here, Peter,' she said, knowing that any emotion would be wiped away in the transmission.

'And you should be here,' he said, and she fancied that he might have been flirting with her. If she hadn't seen him on Saturday evening how would she have responded?

'I'm a doctor, not a radio operator,' he added plaintively.

'Isn't the phone working?' she asked. 'You could contact the base on that.'

'But I might get Sally, then,' he said, 'and miss out on hearing your lovely voice.'

She shrank into her seat, unwilling to acknowledge what his voice and words were doing to her senses. True, it was the kind of joking conversation Peter always carried on, and if there had been other staff members in the room they would have put it down to Peter's customary teasing.

'Do you want something?' she said briskly, hoping that he would understand that her decision was made.

'Only to check that the radio is working,' he told her. 'The army fellow thinks he's improved the wiring and we should be able to call base on several different frequencies.'

He'd either got the message or decided that there were other people in the room with her for he became all business from then on, but every syllable he spoke stabbed its way into her heart.

'I'll see you Wednesday,' he concluded when they'd tried the different bands and found them all working. 'Or I could—'

She pictured him hunched over the radio in the hospital at Coorawalla about to say something else, then remembering how often there were other people with her in the radio room.

'I'll see you Wednesday,' he repeated, his voice flat and low.

'No, Peter,' she whispered, but she had shut off the channel and knew that he wouldn't hear it.

At first she had been angry enough to want to face him with her knowledge, but now she had calmed down and accepted that the less she saw of Peter the better. She couldn't bear to see his lips saying things she didn't want to hear.

But she was to hear his voice again and again. The hospital rang with the results of the blood tests, a list of forty-eight representing all the men who had remained on the island.

'Phone them through to Peter,' Jack told her from a mining camp, where he was evacuating an injured workman after a fire in the cook-house.

She lifted the receiver, her fingers stiff with reluctance, and was relieved when Susan answered.

'Grab a pen and I'll give you the results of the blood tests,' she suggested.

'Hang on, I'll get Peter,' Susan replied, foiling her simple plan. 'He has the list of numbers and the corresponding names, and he knows the fellows better than I do.'

Katie nodded. It made sense.

'Hi, Katie!' His voice was soft, the voice of Peter the Playboy in full pursuit!

'Hello, Peter. Here's the list,' she said briskly, ignoring the tremors that fluttered in her chest.

'So businesslike,' he murmured. 'Do I take that as a no?'

'Of course,' she told him, pleased that the decision was now out in the open. 'If you're ready, here's the list.'

'I'd like to explain the complication,' he said quietly. 'It's just that it's not an easy story to tell.'

'I don't want to know,' she snapped. 'I don't want
to discuss it. I don't—'

Want you, she nearly said, but the lie wouldn't
come out.

'Here's the list!' she repeated, unable to say
anything else.

She read through the numbers and gave him each
result, becoming interested in spite of herself. Often
three numbers would come together, all positive for
antibodies, then a scattering of negatives and another
run of positives.

'Are they family members who came together to have
their blood taken?' she asked Peter as the pattern
became more marked.

'I think they could be,' he said, his voice conveying
that he was similarly intrigued. 'If you hold on for a
moment I'll compare the names and numbers.'

She waited, knowing that she was going to miss the
feeling of collaboration Peter provided when he shared
medical information with her.

'Cousins, I'd say, from their names,' he reported, and
she could sense his excitement. 'I'll have to get one of
the elders in here to unravel the relationships, but it
could be through their maternal line. Oh, Katie,
wouldn't it be wonderful if the immunity was passed
on? A link like that could lead halfway to developing
a vaccine.'

She was unable to stop a smiling response but her
mind was so confused that she wanted to scream. Every
time she tried to classify Peter as a worthless philan-
derer, he did something kind or generated a new
work-orientated excitement in her.

Maybe she would ask him about the blonde—about
the complications.

And maybe she wouldn't!

CHAPTER TEN

KATIE was still debating the choice ahead of her when she reached the airport on Friday morning. Caltura lay ahead of her today—the place where she would be expected to sit on a horse! Would Peter be accompanying her, or would she have to admit her fear to Jack, Caltura's regular clinic doctor, and ask him to hold the horse? Actually, she was so tired that she didn't think she'd care if the horse bit or kicked her. What was a little more pain in her life?

She looked around and, not seeing any familiar faces, walked slowly towards the plane. The crew returning from Coorawalla had been rested yesterday as they had not arrived home until very late on Wednesday evening.

'I phoned you last night.'

She spun around to see Peter standing behind her. He must have been in the hangar when she'd driven in. She moved a step closer, and saw him more clearly. He was looking even more tired than she felt. Her arms lifted from her sides to draw him close before she remembered that what hadn't really started between them was now finished.

'I was called to the animal refuge,' she said, meaning only to explain where she'd been.

'So I heard,' he said flatly. 'With Richard, your mother said. Is that why you look exhausted?'

She was so shocked by the words, by his linking her with Richard, that she lifted her head to look him directly at him.

His eyes were darker, but carefully expressionless.

165

'I realised then that you meant it when you said no on the phone the other day.'

'I didn't exactly say no,' she muttered at him, disconcerted by his blank-faced scrutiny. 'Not right then! And Richard picked me up because he's the person who phoned and asked me to help. A dog had got in under the fence and savaged the wallabies and an elderly kangaroo that live in the compound.'

She saw a tiny flicker come to life in his eyes. Maybe a semi-medical conversation could ease things between them.

'Actually, we could have done with some extra assistance. If I look tired it's because we've been up most of the night, trying to patch up five injured animals and then convince them that they can still trust the people who caged them.'

'And does this tender-hearted approach only extend to animals?'

Again she was shocked by the shading of his words, but Christa had joined them and Bill, their pilot, was calling them to board the plane. Peter moved immediately, leading the way.

'You look all ready for the action,' Christa said, surveying Katie's 'western' outfit of jeans and a not-too-loud checked shirt.

'I was warned about this Stampede,' Katie told her. 'And about the party afterwards. I'm glad you'll be there to support me.'

'It used to be great fun and then the tradition died out for a while, but Andrew Walsh, who's the new health worker and driving force about the place, is determined to get it going again.'

She followed Katie up the steps and into the plane, still talking.

'It's like a rodeo. All the same events—calf-roping,

buck-jumping, bull-riding. The Caltura Stampede is the name it's given—taken from the Calgary Stampede, I suppose!'

'Do you want to run through the patient files with me on the way?' Peter asked Christa. 'You know these people.'

He waved Christa into a seat in front of his, then added, 'You might as well sit up front with Bill, Katie. See something of the countryside.'

She made her way through to the cockpit, feeling decidedly snubbed and unable to follow Peter's ever-changing moods.

Caltura welcomed them with heat and flies and dust. Katie watched Christa bound out of the plane, to be greeted by a handsome man in his mid-thirties. It was only a handshake, but something of the love which had sparkled in the air at Wyrangi seemed to be alive and well here also.

'So that's Andrew Walsh, Caltura's attraction,' Peter murmured behind her and she stumbled on the steps, shocked that he might now be reading her thoughts.

He reached out to steady her, and still held her arm in a light clasp when they reached the gravel runway.

'We go to work now,' he said, 'and you'll be whisked away to socialise, but the offer of holding the horse still stands, Katie.'

His voice was as deep as the rivulets of desire that the oh-so-light touch had generated.

'I'll see you later in the day.'

It was impossible to argue—impossible to avoid him! They were fellow workers, bound together by their love for the Service.

She nodded, and pulled her wide-brimmed hat further down on her forehead so that he wouldn't see the unhappiness in her eyes and smiled.

'OK!' she said lightly, and walked across to where a group of aboriginal women stood chattering beside a battered old Jeep.

They welcomed her with such genuine warmth that she forgot about Peter, and gave herself up to the delights of the day. While preliminary rodeo events were under way, she was shown the 'art school'. Tree-trunks held up a roof of bark and leafy branches, which was high enough to let air circulate but provided ample shade from the burning sun. There, men worked on traditional paintings while women spun reeds and grasses between their palms, lengthening them into threads to weave into baskets and dilly bags.

'Chainsaw on next,' an excited child cried as he ran through the shaded area.

'Chainsaw?'

The woman who had appointed herself spokesperson for the group smiled at her.

'You don't know Chainsaw?' she said, her dark eyes glistening with delight. 'The famous bull?'

Katie shook her head.

'Is he like the rodeo clowns?' she asked, remembering from television how two men worked the rodeo rings, attracting the excited animals away from fallen participants.

'Like that, only a bull,' the woman told her. 'A big white bull. He goes to all the rodeos and all the boys, they try to ride him. If you stay on Chainsaw then you're the best,' she finished simply, and led the way towards the stockyards where a buzz of excitement was heralding the arrival of the star.

'I won't hold Chainsaw while you have a photo taken.'

Peter's voice made her spin around. He was smiling

but, like hers, his hat was pulled well down and she couldn't read his eyes.

'I didn't know there were famous bulls,' she whispered, as the excitement all around her made her forget his 'complication'.

'City girl!' he teased, and her heart leapt at the tenderness in his voice.

As they drew closer to the stockyards Katie saw that a rickety-looking stand had been erected, but most of the viewing public were perched on the stock rails.

'Do you want to sit in the stands, or join the locals on the fence?' he asked.

She looked around for her guide, and couldn't see her.

'I'll join the locals on the fence,' she said, then wondered if that had been a wise move when Peter climbed briskly up the two lower rails and perched precariously on the top one, while he reached down a helping hand.

'I'll manage,' she told him, not wanting to feel his warmth again.

From her vantage point she could look across to where an assortment of trucks and trailers were parked.

'It's like a travelling circus,' she murmured to Peter.

'Complete with its own star,' he told her, pointing to a large, shiny rig right at the back. A huge white bull was painted on the sides of the trailer.

'Chainsaw's travelling hotel?' she asked.

An excited roar drowned Peter's response. She turned to see a man reach out to open a chute, and a thousand pounds of muscled fury careened into the yard.

Katie held her breath, spellbound by the majesty and strength of the beast they called Chainsaw. He cast the man who'd dared to sit on his back flying through the air, but she didn't even turn her head to see if the rider had been hurt. Her heart and soul were bound up in the beauty of the animal, and she sensed that he enjoyed the show-off antics which had the crowd roaring its approval.

She turned to Peter, laughter bubbling on her lips.

'He's an old ham,' she declared delightedly. 'He loves it!'

'Shh,' Peter whispered back, as if binding her into an intimate conspiracy. 'He doesn't want everyone to know it!'

She chuckled and lost her balance on the rail, teetering forward towards the dusty ring. Peter's hand reached out around her waist to catch her, and her breathing stopped as she felt her body respond voraciously to his touch.

For a moment all the noise and dust and laughter faded, and they might have been alone in the world.

'Perhaps it's as well you said no, Katie,' he murmured, 'because I don't think slow and steady ever stood a chance with us, did it?'

He sounded sad and she turned to look at him, then saw his eyes and the emptiness made her look away again.

In the ring two men in baggy clowns' trousers were leading a now-docile Chainsaw towards a gate, and another brave soul was getting ready to drop onto his back and test his reputation.

She wanted to ask Peter so many things, but every time they started to talk one of them got angry, and sitting on a rail above even a mock-enraged bull was no place to be getting emotional.

Four men tried to ride the champion and four men failed, but the crowd applauded their courage and shouted their admiration for Chainsaw.

'Come on, I'll take you over to the hospital,' Christa called to her when the crowds started drifting away. 'We girls are allotted the store-room as our private boudoir. The sooner we get over there the less chance of having to queue for a shower. You've no idea the people who find their way into hospital when the Stampede's on.'

Peter jumped lightly to the ground but, to Katie, the red dust looked too far away and she turned to use the rails as a ladder to climb back down. Thinking about the sport she'd seen and showers and Peter, she missed the second railing and slithered hard against the fence, hanging helplessly until strong arms reached out and caught her then held her close for a moment, before lowering her feet gently to the ground.

His hands steadied her, and she felt his fingers trembling on her skin.

'Come on,' Christa called again, turning back to see where she was.

'I'll see you later, Katie,' Peter murmured, and she knew that she wasn't going to be strong enough to stem the tide of desire sweeping through her.

Could she forget what she had seen on Saturday night? Forget the word 'free' she thought she'd painfully unscrambled from the stuck-together pieces of letter?

Was it possible to seize whatever happiness Peter could give her, turning her back on doubt and suspicion? Living for the moment and letting the future take care of itself?

She plodded after Christa, head bent, watching the little puffs of dust that flew up around her feet with every step she took.

Happiness would be as ephemeral as that dust, she heard her father's voice whisper in her head, if taken at the expense of someone else.

'Here we are!'

She looked up to see Christa waving her towards a

door leading off a wide-roofed verandah.

'Our bedroom awaits us. Peter dropped your overnight bag in here earlier.'

Katie looked around with interest. Only months ago this 'hospital' had been an old abandoned school building, but Andrew Walsh had swept into Caltura and miracles had begun.

'The shower's outside, but there's a bit of corrugated iron around it for privacy. Do you want to go first?'

'You go ahead,' she told Christa, wanting to be alone for a few minutes while she tried to find a solution to the tormenting thoughts and tantalising desires which were tearing her apart.

'The first thing to do is find out about the complication,' she said aloud, stepping over a narrow bed to get at her overnight bag.

'I agree, and I'm here to tell you all about it.'

She started with fright, grabbed at her bag and fell back onto the bed, bringing a stack of cardboard boxes tumbling down from the shelves. The boxes opened as they fell, cascading the contents all over the floor, the bed and her shaking body.

'You shouldn't sneak up on people like that!' she said to Peter, turning towards the door of the small room and glaring at him.

'I didn't sneak,' he said, and seemed about to say something else when his eyes lit with joy. He shook his head and advanced far enough into the room to shut the door behind him.

'So, what's to stop us this time, Katie, my love?' he murmured, and she could see his shoulders shaking with a secret mirth.

'What are you talking about?' she demanded as her heart reacted to his approach with a rapid acceleration.

'I mean this and this and this,' he said, scooping up

handfuls of the boxes' contents and scattering them around her on the bed. 'Safe sex, Katie darling,' he added, dropping onto the bed beside her and taking her into his arms.

'You are sitting in a sea of condoms,' he whispered, then pressed his lips to hers, catching her choke of embarrassment and turning it into a sigh of greedy satisfaction.

This is wrong, wrong, wrong, her mind tried to tell her, but it was such bliss to be in Peter's arms and, with Christa due back from the shower at any moment, it couldn't lead to too much trouble.

'We have dinner, then a dance,' he paused long enough to tell her. 'They will spread us out around the different tables, but later I will dance with you and try to explain about. . .my family.'

The words crunched underneath her joy, like broken glass under a heavy tread, then Christa returned—to find Peter and Katie both kneeling on the floor and pushing slim foil packets feverishly back into boxes.

'Needed a few did you, Peter?' Christa teased, and Katie, scarlet with embarrassment, tried to explain how she'd knocked them down.

She dressed for the dinner in a light, crinkle-cotton skirt and matching halter-neck top. The swirling pattern of blues and greens made her skin look paler and brought out the green in her eyes, but she barely noticed her appearance as excitement waxed and waned within her.

'Told you it wasn't too bright,' Peter whispered in her ear when she and Christa entered the crowded community hall. She looked around and smiled at the colourful clothes of both sexes. Men in bright checked cowboy shirts and string ties escorted their wives and girlfriends in flowing caftans or skimpy sun-frocks—

all rioting with reds and pinks, deep greens and vivid electric blue.

Katie smiled.

'It's like walking into a wonderful spring garden,' she murmured back, relishing the feel of Peter's hand resting lightly against the small of her back.

One of the organisers appeared, and they were led away to places of honour at the tables. Katie was placed next to an elderly artist whom she had met earlier in the day, and the time passed quickly as she listened to his stories of the Dreamtime—the stories he tried to tell in his intricate paintings.

'Dancing after this,' the young man on her other side remarked, nodding towards one end of the hall. 'And riding the bull.'

She looked up and saw a band setting up, but the 'bull' puzzled her.

'I thought you'd all tried that this afternoon?' she said, and saw the quick white flash of his smile.

'Mechanical bull,' he explained with great economy, and she blinked and turned to her older neighbour for an explanation.

'Well, you missed your ride on a horse today; perhaps you'll try the bull,' Peter said, arriving to claim her for the promised dance as soon as dinner and the speeches were over.

She walked over with him towards the ungainly contraption that, to her, looked like a barrel on a heavy spring.

'No, thanks,' she said, eyeing the heavy matting spread out on the floor. 'It looks as if it's designed to throw people off, not keep them on.'

Peter was prodding the mats with his foot.

'It is,' he said. 'Wait here a moment.'

He hurried away, appearing at the other end of the

padded area some time later. He was waving his hands and talking volubly to a small, older man who appeared to be in charge. The man nodded and then as more mats appeared Peter directed their disposal, thickening the layer of padding which surrounded the machine.

'I hate these things,' Peter muttered, reappearing like a genie by her side. 'They fill me with foreboding.'

'But are they more dangerous than the real bulls the young men rode today?'

'Probably not,' Peter admitted, easing her through the growing crowd around the bull, 'which doesn't make me feel any better.'

He led the way to where the dancing had started and, with a sigh, took her gently in his arms.

'Not as close as I'd like to hold you,' he said, looking down into her face and smiling, 'but it's a bit early in the evening for smooching on the dance-floor.'

She knew that she was blushing because she could feel the heat in her cheeks, but that was a minor problem compared to the other effects of Peter's touch. Her body had lightened until she floated over the floor, and her head spun with the magic of his hand holding hers. Such a simple thing—to dance together—yet magically special.

She was so absorbed in cataloguing her own delight that she didn't hear him begin to speak, and only became aware that he was talking when the band stopped for a moment before picking up a different tune.

'I'm sorry, Peter, I missed that,' she said, looking up at him in order to concentrate on his words.

But the movement of his lips mesmerised her again, and she caught only snippets of the explanation—about a sister, and attendant care, and funding, and autism, and—

'What did you say you did on Saturday nights?' she

demanded, as the snippets joined themselves together to make a vague kind of sense.

'I take care of my sister, who is autistic,' he said, looking gravely down into her face. 'Do you know what that means?'

'What autistic means? Or what her autism means in terms of the care she needs?' Katie snapped. 'It doesn't matter because I know both, and I also know that people with disabilities are people first and foremost and that's how they should be considered. Too many people think in terms of their disability rather than their ability— and to think that you. . .'

They had stopped dancing and were facing each other in the centre of the dance-floor.

He shook his head and smiled, his eyes alight with something that looked like love.

'Katie—collector of stray animals—I should have known!'

But Katie wasn't over her anger.

'I can't believe this!' she stormed. 'Are you telling me your sister is the other complication in your life? A *complication*! Your sister? Your own flesh and blood? And you've hidden her away like some dark secret—because if anyone at that base knew about this we would all have known? I don't believe this, Peter; I don't believe you!'

She shook off the hand which still rested on her shoulder, and walked swiftly away, aware that the little scene was attracting more than its share of attention.

'Katie!'

He caught up with her as she reached the wide concreted area outside the hall, and turned her towards him.

'Are you yelling at me because I didn't care enough about Jenny to tell everyone—because you thought I was ashamed of her—was hiding her?'

'Of course I am,' she choked out. 'I can't believe I could have fallen in love with someone so. . .so insensitive!'

'Fallen in love with?' The words were the barest whisper, as if saying them aloud might break some spell. 'Oh, Katie!'

The last words were a triumphant shout as he seized her and swung her into his arms, twirling her around and around in the air until the world tilted alarmingly when he set her down again.

Or was it just that she was in his arms again and his lips were brushing against her hair?

'Let me explain,' he said, and led her to where low-slung canvas chairs were backed against the wall, deep in shadow—private and secluded.

He sat down and drew her onto his knee.

'Jenny was only ten when my mother became ill. At that age she needed constant supervision and my parents decided she should go into a hostel that specialised in autism.'

Peter paused, then spoke again.

'In fact, now I've thought back over a lot of things that were happening then I think that probably my father decided and Mum was too sick to argue. I was put into boarding-school and Mum explained that Jenny was in a similar school.'

His arms tightened and he rocked her on his knee for a moment, as if the memories were hurting him.

'When Mum died my father said it was best for Jenny to stay where she was—that she had friends there—that she would be looked after properly—that it was best for her. I probably believed his theory because it made things easier for us all,' he said, his voice hoarse and rasping. 'I was sixteen, and having a daffy sister wasn't exactly cool!' Bitterness grazed the words.

Katie turned in his arms so that she could hold him and drew his head against her shoulder, running her fingers through the thick, gold-streaked thatch of hair.

'You were sixteen, Peter,' she repeated. 'You believed it because your father told you—not for any other reason. And what else could you have done? Could you have cared for her yourself? Helped her through the adolescent years, which are extremely difficult for people with autism?'

His head lifted and he kissed her, very gently, on the lips, and again he breathed her name as if in wonder that she could understand.

'Did you keep in touch? Did your father bring her home for holidays?'

Peter nodded.

'Maybe he honestly believed it was for the best,' he admitted, 'because he did visit her, and took me when I wasn't caught up in school or studies. At Christmas he'd employ a carer, and she would come home for a fortnight.'

There was another pause, as if he was gathering the strength for the next revelation.

'And I grew to hate those fortnights,' he said sadly, 'because she was so restless. She would wander around the house day and night, touching things, her beautiful face so puzzled it made me ache all through.'

'She has no speech?' Katie asked, remembering a similar friend with severe autism and the face of a Botticelli angel.

'No, but she was trying to tell us something.'

He sighed again and his hands rubbed up and down along her arms as if he might be cold and warming the wrong person.

'And I ignored it. All through university I told myself she was in the best possible place—that my father knew best. I studied all I could find on the subject and debated the newer theories that people with challenging behaviour should be helped to live normal lives in the community. What's normal? I would say, and give examples of Jenny stripping off her clothes in a supermarket—at fourteen and fully developed! I could even make a joke of it.'

'And your father?'

'I never questioned how he felt,' Peter admitted. 'Even as an adolescent, when I should have been questioning his values—to test my own theories if for no other reason—I clung blindly to his edicts. Two of them! Doctors should marry late, and Jenny was better off in care—the pair twisted together like the strands of a piece of rope. I refused to get deeply involved with anyone because, I realise now, to question one of those edicts would mean I had to question the other.'

'And now?' Katie whispered.

'For the last three years—since I've been up here— I've had less time to visit Jenny, but it was like an aching tooth, Katie, nagging away inside my head. I began to wonder about my motives in coming north— to wonder if I was trying to break away from her. I spoke to my father, who remained adamant that he was right and pointed out that there were no options—that I couldn't take care of her. Then, at Christmas, I flew down to visit her, and I knew I couldn't let her live like that any longer.'

'Live like what?' she asked, remembering horror stories of old-fashioned institutions.

'Oh, it was a lovely place,' Peter assured her, 'and the carers and attendants were well trained and kindly, but they were treating her like a child and even I could see the frustration building inside her. She had temper tantrums, they said, and, watching her fling a colouring-book across the room, I suddenly understood why. She needed more stimulation, more company and, particularly, more adult pursuits.'

'So?'

'So, I asked her if she would like to live near me. She flung herself into my arms, and I knew it was right. I packed her up, there and then, and brought her north with me, then realised that my erratic work pattern was hardly conducive to caring for someone who needs twenty-four-hours-a-day supervision.'

'Did you find the organisations that arrange attendant care, and help people like Jenny live independently?'

He hugged her, as if unable to believe that she actually knew about such things.

'Through Jack, who does know about Jenny, I discovered a world of wonderful people who seem to exist solely to help others. She now lives in a flat with another girl, but the funding doesn't allow for a carer at weekends so she comes home to me on Saturday morning and goes back to the flat on Sunday evening.'

He paused for a moment, and then he said, 'I wasn't keeping her a secret, Katie, although it must seem that way. When I first came north the only way I could handle my doubts was by pretending that everything was fine, and, since she's been here, I've been getting to know her all over again and helping her adjust to a huge change in her life. It's been a difficult process for both of us—and a private thing we had to do together. . .'

'I can understand that,' Katie assured him, hearing the guilt which still burdened his heart. She remembered him talking about his mother and wondered about the traumatic effect which her lingering illness and death had had on the teenage boy. In his grief and loneliness he would have had to believe in his father—or lose what little he had left.

'And the other edict?' she asked, knowing that she had to finish this conversation.

He drew her deeper into his arms and kissed her gently, then traced his fingers across her face as he spoke again.

'I'm beginning to believe that I didn't question that one because there was no need to—because I hadn't fallen in love with the one woman who could make me question it.'

He kissed her again, pledging something too deep to be put into words. As the heat built within her, Katie knew she had to contain it—knew that this was not the time or the place for the fiery conflagration. She pushed away a little and dragged air into her lungs.

Think of something else!

'Would you like to have Jenny live permanently with you?' she asked, trying to distract her body's wanton hunger.

To her surprise, he accepted the diversion and chuckled.

'No,' he said firmly. 'It took me far too long to embrace the new philosophy, but I think I've finally got a grasp on it. Don't you realise it's just as "un-normal" for a grown women to live for ever with her brother—and hopefully, one day, her brother's family—as it is for her to live for ever as a child?'

His lips teased at hers again, inflammatory and inciting.

'Was that all too much to dump on you at once?' he murmured. 'And did you hear the bit about "her brother's family"?'

She met his kiss and forgot about time and place,

responding with all the passion she had bottled up within her heart.

'Are you there, Peter?'

Christa's voice! With urgency ringing in its tones.

Peter stood up swiftly, setting Katie on the floor and brushing his hand across her hair.

'Coming!' he called back, and she thought she could hear a tremor of emotion in the word.

'There's never time to finish things,' he said, frustration making the words seem harsh. 'Don't slip away from me again, Katie!'

He was gone before she could reply and she followed more slowly, hearing whispers of conversations that told of a young man thrown off the bucking machine.

Someone reached out and pulled her up onto the stage, and she looked down to see Peter crouched over the fallen youngster.

'There's a blue metal stretcher on the plane,' he said, turning to Andrew Walsh, who crouched beside him. 'And a cervical collar in one of the equipment bags. Take Christa, she'll know where to find them, and tell Bill we should fly direct to Brisbane. That way this chap can go straight into a spinal unit. His neck could be broken and the less we transfer him the better.'

As Katie watched with a chilled fascination Peter remained where he was, holding the young man's head with steady hands. It seemed an age before Andrew returned, and she saw Christa pull the stretcher into two pieces. Peter fastened the collar around the patient's neck then supervised the helpers, who were sliding the two pieces under the prone body.

Once the stretcher was snapped back together again willing helpers lifted it and, with Peter's hands still keeping the head immobile, the little procession walked slowly out of the room.

The band struck up again, a quieter tune, and Katie danced with strangers until Christa reappeared.

'They've gone,' she said quietly. 'Peter went with them, and I was told to stay behind to keep you company. Jack will arrange for someone to fly us home tomorrow.'

'I wasn't worried about getting home,' Katie said honestly. 'In fact, I'd forgotten I couldn't get in my car and drive away.'

Christa looked at her strangely, and they walked over to their store-room 'quarters' in silence.

The morning of the quest finals arrived—a bright clear Saturday which showed promise of cooler weather with a sharpness in the breeze that blew in from the sea.

Katie knew that she wouldn't be chosen Queen of the Outback. That honour would rightfully go to one of the women who had worked hard all year to raise money for the RFDS, but she might be Charity Queen— thanks to a sizeable, last-minute donation from Alex Solano.

She was sitting on the front step, watching her mother prune back the heavy summer growth in the garden, when the rattle of a sports car engine sent her heart whirling into madness.

'Good-morning, Mrs Watson. Good morning, my queen,' Peter greeted them, bounding up the path towards her with a pile of boxes balanced in his outstretched arms.

She blushed, as she always did, at Peter's exuberant and open expression of his love for her. It was all too new, too wonderful—too unbelievable—for her to accept with any equanimity.

'What have you got there?' she asked, trying to pretend that she was more interested in the packages than she was in the sight of his strong physique and gleaming, golden good looks.

'Presents!' he announced. 'Mostly for you, but this one's for your mother.'

He placed them on the verandah floor beside her, lifted a small box off the top and took it across to her mother with a courtly flourish.

'White orchids! Oh, Peter, they are lovely!'

Katie watched as her mother slipped an arm around Peter's neck and kissed him on the cheek. Tears smarted in her eyes as she realised what he had missed through his mother's early death. Could she, and her close and loving family, heal those wounds he still kept hidden?

'Tears?' he asked, lifting her chin and inspecting her eyes.

'Only happy ones,' she assured him, and met his kiss with all the power of the silent pledge she had just made.

'I think,' he whispered huskily a little later, 'now this Queen business will be finished tonight we should make wedding plans.'

Katie looked down at the emerald ring which still sparkled newly on her finger.

'Won't people think we're rushing things?' she teased.

'Of course they will,' he answered her, capturing her hand and kissing it. 'But they know I'm wild and impetuous.'

Katie blushed again, and looked up shyly to see a wash of colour in Peter's cheeks. The heat of their passion still rocked them both—a burning wave that could sweep them to unbelievable heights then leave them spent and drained, unable to put into words the magnitude of their physical love.

'I've got to collect Jenny,' he said, but she could

see the desire one look had fired, already burning in his eyes.

'Yes,' she agreed, answering both his words and the longing.

He bent and kissed her swiftly, then he was gone.

'Are you going to open your parcels?' her mother asked.

Katie stared at her mother, then remembered the parcels. She'd been lost in an erotic dream of. . .

'I should have bought that silk dress,' she said, suddenly dissatisfied with the formal evening gown she'd decided would 'do' for tonight!

'There's time to go into town,' her mother reminded her, but she hesitated.

If Peter had liked it he would have ordered her to take it, she decided, remembering, with a smile, how bossy he had been about her clothes. Now he seemed to prefer her without any, she thought, then coloured again at her boldness.

'I'm going to write a thank you speech in case I'm Charity Queen,' she told her mother, determining to return to her sensible and practical self once again. This love business had sent her into a most un-Katie-like spin.

She carried the boxes through to her bedroom and opened them.

The top one, smallest of all, held an emerald pendant which made her fingers tremble just holding it. The next she opened gingerly and found a pair of sheer black stockings, lace topped and so sexy they took her breath away. Until she found the suspender belt—a froth of black satin and tiny green ribbons!

'Oh, Peter!' she breathed, then lifted the lid on the last gift.

The gown had been packed in tissue, so that when

she pulled it out and shook it gently the creases fell away. She spread it on the bed, seeing the richness of the dark green silk against her white bedcover, and reached for the note that lay beneath it.

I began to wonder if I loved you when I saw you in this dress. At least, I knew enough to know that I didn't want anyone else looking at you in it. You were—and are—so beautiful!

But, now you are mine, I find I want to show you off and to shout to the world that I love you! Wear it for me, Katie!

She had read it through three times before she realised that reading his writing had not been an intellectual challenge. She looked again and realised that he had printed it! This time there could be no mistake about what he was saying—about what he felt.

The applause finally died away, and Katie made her way back to the table where her friends from the base and her parents were seated. As she sat down next to Peter the ethereally lovely blonde, in a gown of ice blue, reached out and touched her hand, and then her face.

She covered the fine-boned hand with hers and looked into the beautiful blue eyes.

'Are you enjoying yourself, Jenny?' she asked softly, knowing not to expect a response.

'Of course she is,' Christa answered. 'She's danced with every man at this table, and has more rhythm and grace than any of us.'

And Jenny smiled.

Katie knew that it could have been coincidence, but there was no denying that the young woman seemed happy to be with them. Katie reached under the table and squeezed Peter's hand—which seemed to be toying with the catch on her suspender belt!

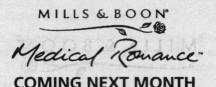

MILLS & BOON®

Medical Romance™

COMING NEXT MONTH

MISLEADING SYMPTOMS by Lilian Darcy
Camberton Hospital

How could Dr Megan Stone work with Dr Callum Priestley again, when she couldn't forget the night they had shared two years previously? Callum behaved as if nothing had happened, but now Megan really wanted him to see her as more than a colleague...

OUTLOOK—PROMISING! by Abigail Gordon
Springfield Community Hospital

Dr Rachel Maddox needed a quiet life after her divorce, and her new job and home seemed ideal—until Nicholas Page, eminent neuro-surgeon, began involving her in his life, and trying to organise hers!

HEART SURGEON by Josie Metcalfe
St Augustine's Hospital

Sister Helen Morrisey's sole aim was to be part of surgeon Noah Kincaid's team, because only then did she have a chance of regaining her small son from the Middle East. But she'd forgotten something important, and Noah offered to smooth her path—but what did he gain?

SISTER SUNSHINE by Elisabeth Scott
Kids & Kisses

Widower Dr Adam Brent was sure Sister Julie Maynard wouldn't cope with the job, but she proved him wrong, charming the patients, his two small children—and Adam! But he still wasn't prepared for commitment...

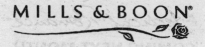

MILLS & BOON®

Marry me COWBOY

When your lover is a cowboy...

You'll have a stetson on the bedpost and boots under the bed.

And you'll have a man who's hard-living, hard-loving and sexy as hell to keep you warm all night...every night!

Watch it happen in these four delightful new stories by your favourite authors—
Janet Dailey,
Margaret Way, Susan Fox and Anne McAllister

Available:May 1997   Price: £4.99

MILLS & BOON®

To Have & To Hold

Celebrate the joy, excitement and sometimes
mishaps that occur when planning that special
wedding in our treasured four-story collection.

Written by four talented authors—
Barbara Bretton, Rita Clay Estrada,
Sandra James and Debbie Macomber

Don't miss this wonderful short story collection
for incurable romantics everywhere!

Available: April 1997   Price: £4.99

KEEPING COUNT

How would you like to win a year's supply of Mills & Boon® books? Well you can and they're FREE! Simply complete the competition below and send it to us by 31st October 1997. The first five correct entries picked after the closing date will each win a year's subscription to the Mills & Boon series of their choice. What could be easier?

$$6 + 3 + \boxed{} = 14$$

$$\boxed{} + 2 + \boxed{} = 15$$

$$\boxed{} + 1 + \boxed{} = 16$$

$$\boxed{} + 6 + \boxed{} = 17$$

$$\boxed{} + 3 + \boxed{} = 18$$

$$\boxed{} + 1 + \boxed{} = 19$$

$$\boxed{} + 5 + \boxed{} = 20$$

C7D

PLEASE TURN OVER FOR DETAILS OF HOW TO ENTER ☞

How to enter...

There are six sets of numbers overleaf. When the first empty box has the correct number filled into it, then that set of three numbers will add up to 14. All you have to do, is figure out what the missing number of each of the other five sets are so that the answer to each will be as shown. The first number of each set of three will be the last number of the set before. Good Luck!

When you have filled in all the missing numbers don't forget to fill in your name and address in the space provided and tick the Mills & Boon® series you would like to receive if you are a winner. Then simply pop this page into an envelope (you don't even need a stamp) and post it today. Hurry, competition ends 31st October 1997.

Mills & Boon 'Keeping Count' Competition
FREEPOST, Croydon, Surrey, CR9 3WZ

Eire readers send competition to PO Box 4546, Dublin 24

Please tick the series you would like to receive if you are a winner
Presents™ ❏ Enchanted™ ❏ Temptation® ❏
Medical Romance™ ❏ Historical Romance™ ❏

Are you a Reader Service Subscriber? Yes ❏ No ❏

Ms/Mrs/Miss/Mr_____

(BLOCK CAPS PLEASE)

Address _____

_____

_____ Postcode_____

(I am over 18 years of age)

C7D